Protecting Lindsay

Elsa Winckler

Protecting Lindsay
Copyright © 2022 Elsa Winckler
All rights reserved.

ISBN: (ebook) 978-1-953335-94-4
(print) 978-1-953335-95-1

Inkspell Publishing
207 Moonglow Circle #101
Murrells Inlet, SC 29576

Edited By Rie Langdon
Cover Art By Fantasia Frog

DEDICATION

To my granddaughter, Alannah

ELSA WINCKLER

CHAPTER 1

"And you're sure this will, um…" Suzie Stevens looked around her before she continued in a whisper. "Help…my Donald to…you know, get it up?"

The problem was, Suzie's whisper could be heard all the way over at Alisson High School.

Swallowing the giggle wanting desperately to escape, Lindsay tried to look suitably grave. For Suzie, what happened in her bedroom was a serious business. "If the doctor has declared your husband fit and healthy, this could do the trick. But as I've explained, you don't drink this, you use the contents for massaging. It's fractionated coconut oil with drops of ylang-ylang, orange, ginger, black pepper, and patchouli essential oils. And this," she held up the smaller bottle, "you use in your diffuser as I've shown you. This is a mixture of tangerine, bergamot, ylang-ylang, sandalwood, cedarwood—"

Behind her, the bell rang and the door opened. Her whole body stiffened, and in that moment she knew exactly who had entered her shop. Blake Davidson. She didn't have to turn around to know it was him. The tingle down her spine was confirmation enough. Unfortunately, Lilly, her assistant, had already left for the day; otherwise she might have had a warning.

The last time she'd seen him was nearly two months ago at her sister Charlie's wedding. How he'd ended up being one of Logan's groomsmen, she still hadn't been able to figure out. She hadn't known he and Logan had become friends.

Before the wedding, he'd been gone for about a month and he'd disappeared again immediately afterwards. Since then, she hadn't heard anything from him. He'd opened a dojo in town earlier this year, and she and Charlie had been to a few of his self-defense classes.

But then they'd received a message he'd be out of town for a while—someone else would be teaching his classes. That was at the point where her own life had begun to fall apart, and neither she nor Charlie had been back for another class.

So she'd noticed he was gone. Well, not really noticed. It wasn't as if she was thinking about him, but...

"Lindsay?" Suzie asked, and Lindsay realized she'd stopped mid-sentence.

"Uhm..." She looked down at the bottle in her hand and nearly groaned out loud. To be talking about spicing up the bedroom, of all things, when Blake was standing behind her—seriously? Talking a deep breath, she continued, "Vanilla and manuka essential oils."

Suzie was beaming. "I've never heard of any of those, but if they can help my Donald, I'm willing to try it." Again, she looked furtively around her and when she spotted Blake, she tried her whisper again. "So where do I put it?"

Desperately, Lindsay swallowed the hysterical laughter threatening to escape while she willed the heat creeping up her neck to disappear. Goodness, who still blushed at twenty-six? She lowered her voice. "You can apply it to the inner wrists, the lower back, behind the ears, your neck, and the inner thighs, lower abdomen."

Grinning, Suzie leaned forward. "The thighs?" Her

eyes twinkled. "Well, dear, I like that idea." Again, her whisper was loud enough to be heard all over town.

At this point Lindsay had to turn around. Without directly looking at Blake, she nodded in his direction. "Hi, Blake. Are you looking for me?" Her heart did its usual happy skip-and-a-jump, as it seemed compelled to do whenever the blasted man was near her.

"Yes."

Typical Blake reaction. He never used more than one word if he could help it.

"Just a moment." The silly movements of her heart she would simply ignore, as she'd been doing ever since the night she'd met him. So far, it had worked.

Lindsay walked towards the till, Suzie hot on her heels.

"And I can phone you if this doesn't work?" Suzie wanted to know.

Lindsay smiled as she rang up the transaction and put the items in a bag. "You're a beautiful woman, Suzie." Lindsay smiled. "Be you—that's all you need to do," she said encouragingly.

"You really think so?" Suzie asked, patting her hair.

Seeing the uncertainty in the older woman's eyes, Lindsay took her hand and led her to the mirror against the wall. "Look at those legs and your high cheekbones? Women spend a lot of money trying to get this look, but you already have it."

Suzie turned to her, smiling. "Really?"

Lindsay smiled and nodded. "Really." She handed her the package. "Let me know how it goes." She winked. And with a giggle, Suzie finally left the shop.

It was after five and the sun had already set. It was the beginning of November and although Alisson winters were mild in comparison to the rest of Montana, this time of day temperatures dropped. It was cold and Lindsay wanted to get home.

It was Friday, the end of a long week, and she couldn't wait to be on her own. She loved her customers, but after a busy few days, she needed some alone time to recharge. Introvert problems, her sister, Charlie, called it.

With a last wave in Suzie's direction, she turned back to Blake. He was standing near one of the counters, hands in pockets, clearly not feeling too comfortable amidst her oils and creams and Christmas decorations.

For the first time, she really looked at him. Oh, my. He'd grown a beard since she'd last seen him. She'd never liked beards, but on this tall, dark, and ridiculously attractive guy, it only added to his smoldering good looks.

Grinding her teeth to make sure her jaw wouldn't drop, she turned away. "So, which essential oils are you interested in buying today?"

Here she was, a grown woman, just about salivating because a gorgeous man was in her shop. Maybe she should seriously begin to think about dating again. "There is an essential oil for just about every problem you may have. Suzie's husband, for instance…" The minute the words left her mouth, Lindsay nearly groaned out loud. Normally, she kept clients' issues completely confidential, but Suzie had already let that cat way out of the bag. Even so, why talk about Suzie's bedroom problem, of all things, while she was talking to Blake?

"I don't have problems in the bedroom." His voice was as smooth as Tennessee whiskey.

Lindsay closed her eyes for a minute. He didn't have to tell her that; one look at his broad shoulders, square jaw, and confident stride made it clear he was all man and… Oh, my goodness, the very last thing she should be thinking about was Blake and bedrooms.

"Okay, so maybe something for your beard?" Why didn't she simply shut up? She motioned to one of the shelves. "I make a very nice oil with lavender, peppermint, lemon, and coconut oil. You should try it."

"I don't…" he began gruffly, before he swore softly and took out his wallet. "Okay, give me the damn oil."

She took a bottle down and walked towards the till.

4

"Anything else?"

"No," he said tersely and paid her.

She gave him the package and turned away. She began to clear the counters and checked whether all the cupboards were closed.

"Can you stand still for one damn minute?" Blake growled. "I want to talk to you."

"I have to finish here; I want to go home. It's been a long day and I'm hungry."

"Great. So am I. I'll take you out to dinner."

Exasperated, she looked at him. When had he moved so close to her? "I have food…"

"In that case, you can feed me." And moving away, he began closing the shutters at the windows.

"Blake, seriously…" she began hotly, but he ignored her.

"I mentioned I want to talk to you. So I can either take you to dinner or you can give me dinner—your choice." His voice was clipped; he was clearly in the habit of barking out orders.

She straightened her shoulders. "Well, I don't want to talk to you," she said. Ever since she'd met this man in the local bar earlier that year, he'd been irritating the living daylights out of her. Okay, maybe irritating wasn't the right word. "Bothering" was probably a better description.

He looked at her; something flashed in his eyes, leaving her breathless. She quickly moved towards the cupboards where she kept her bag and jacket. He turned her inside out with just a look, and she didn't like it one bit. "Good day. I'm leaving now."

Clearly exasperated, he rubbed a hand over his face. "Lindsay, damn it, I have to make sure you're safe, I want to—"

"You're my self-defense instructor, that's it. Well, you were before you left, that is." Fed up with him and her stupid fluttering heart, she picked up her bag and jacket. "I haven't been back to the dojo; I'm fine. And I'm not your problem. I don't need looking after, thank you very much. I can do that myself."

"Someone tried to run you down, damn it! Or have you forgotten that?"

Pulling on her jacket, she shrugged. "They've caught the guy, haven't they? Anyway, as I've said, not your problem."

He opened his mouth and closed it again, pressing his lips together.

Maddened, she took the keys of the shop out of her bag and walked towards the door.

"I don't think the guy who's been taken into custody is your real problem, as I think you very well know. I have information you'll want to know about," Blake said from behind her. "It's about Mark Taylor."

Her breath hitched in her throat, and she stopped. "What information?" Slowly, she turned to face him again. Fear threatened to cut off her oxygen, and she had to inhale deeply. Mark Taylor was the guy who'd nearly broken her spirit, and she hated the fact that the mere mention of his name still made her shiver.

"Let's go for dinner and I'll tell you."

Instantly, fear was replaced with irritation. "This is blackmail and you know it. Fine. But just remember this is no date." Turning on her heel, she walked out of the shop.

Blake followed her out. With unsteady fingers, she tried to lock the door but she dropped the keys. Quickly bending forward, she put out her hand to pick it up, but Blake was already reaching out and her fingers encountered his. When she looked up, only a few centimeters separated their faces.

Her breath left her body in one swoosh and for a moment she was unable to move.

"When I ask you out on a date, you'll know it." Chocolate brown eyes darkened.

Inside her, something moved. Rattled, she jumped up and turned away. He'd said "when" he took her on a date, as if it was something that would definitely happen.

Swearing beneath his breath, Blake locked the door to Lindsay's shop. What the hell was wrong with him, talking about dating? He was here to help her, not spook her.

Following her to his car, his eyes glued to her very tantalizing ass, he swore under his breath. Oh, man. His body was still not under control after listening to her explaining to a customer how she could improve things in the bedroom. The very graphic pictures her words had conjured up had given him a few embarrassing moments. Fortunately, both women had been too busy to notice his response.

How the hell had he ended up in this situation? From the moment he'd met Lindsay Wilson at the local bar in June, she'd managed to make him feel things he couldn't allow himself to feel. Ever. With soft, blond hair cascading down her back and eyes the color of the sky on a clear day, she literally took his breath away.

He'd come to Alisson with one clear goal and that was to get away from trouble of any kind. But on the first night he was in town, he'd met this incredibly beautiful woman. She was trouble, he'd known, and that was before he'd heard about her past.

Blake checked the street and made a mental note of the green car parked down the way as he quickened his step to open the door for her. But she'd opened the door already before he could reach it.

"Let me…" he said and opened the door wider.

"Seriously, I can lock and open doors, you know? Been able to since I was three." And with a shake of her head, she got into the car.

Today she was wearing a pair of jeans and boots, but he'd seen those long legs in summer and remembered the satiny, long limbs that were now covered in denim. And although the jacket she was wearing at this moment cloaked most of her body, he also had a vivid memory of a delicate lace top hugging generous curves he couldn't seem to get out of his head.

Lace. She always wore lace. Muted pinks, blues, or yellow, but always lace. Even in this cold, the top underneath her jacket was made of soft pink lace.

He closed her door and muttering and cursing, walked around to the driver's side, again furtively looking at the green car down the street. It hadn't moved and was too far away for him to establish whether anyone was sitting inside.

Taking a deep breath, he got into the car and closed the door. Floral notes of Lindsay's perfume, or whatever the hell she used, floated towards him, sending his already over-stimulated senses into a higher gear. Damn it, this had been such a bad idea.

Pressing his lips together, he switched on the car.

"I don't know why you insist on taking me out to dinner. It's obvious you're not very happy about it. It'll make it much easier for both of us if you simply tell me about Mark and get it over with. There is no need to discuss it over a meal, seriously. And I can get home on my own."

Blake ignored her, put the transmission in gear, and slipped onto the road, driving past the green car. And yes, there was someone inside, all right, but the guy's head was turned away so he couldn't see what he looked like.

When he had passed the parked car, he again checked in the rearview mirror. Now the lights of the car shone brightly. Was the person behind the wheel following them, or was it a coincidence? Blake took out his phone and dialed the local police office's number.

He'd never believed in coincidences. After he'd given them the number plates of the car, he checked again in the mirror. This time, the car wasn't behind them any longer. But he was still uneasy.

"What was that all about?" Lindsay asked, motioning to

his phone.

"Nothing you have to worry about."

"Blake Davidson, so help me…" She inhaled deeply. "I can look after myself; nobody appointed you—"

He stepped on the brake and stopped the car before he made the conscious decision. When he turned to Lindsay, she was very close to him. The space inside the car had shrunk, or so it seemed at the moment.

"I'm worried about your safety," he said.

"Why? You don't even know me!" she cried out.

"Don't you think I know that?" he muttered, his eyes on her lips. She had the most incredible mouth.

"So why…?" she began, but he was done talking.

He had to tell her what he knew, and then get the hell away from her as soon as possible before he did something they would both regret. Putting the car in gear, he stepped on the pedal, glancing in the rearview mirror again. Still no green car.

Beside him, Lindsay was muttering, but he tried his best to ignore her presence. "Bar or restaurant?"

"Restaurant, please. Eleanor and Brooke will probably be at the bar, and if Eleanor sees us together, she'll be organizing a wedding before you know what's hit you."

He drove in silence for a few moments, his brain making giant leaps before he took the next left turn. "Well, then, we'll make it the bar."

"Haven't you heard what I've said?" she asked, clearly annoyed.

"I've heard you. Eleanor is going to think we're a couple. And maybe it's not such a bad idea."

Lindsay looked completely baffled. "You… I … Don't be ridiculous! Why on earth would you say that?"

He parked next to the bar. "Mark Taylor left South Africa a week ago with a plane ticket to Bozeman. He was seen at the airport in Bozeman the next day, but since then nobody knows where he is." And only when he'd finished speaking did he turn to face her.

The lights from the streetlamps outside fell over her, revealing the paleness of her face. Her lips trembled and she put a hand against her mouth. He suppressed the overwhelming urge to take her in his arms and tell her everything would be okay. The two times in his life he'd promised that to someone, things hadn't turned out as planned.

"Your sister and her husband are in Seattle for a month," he continued. "Your brother is back in South Africa, settling his affairs before he returns to Alisson, but it could take months. You live alone at the moment. With Taylor around, I don't think it's safe for you to be on your own. If we're a couple…"

Lindsay looked down at her clenched fists. She was upset and angry but her heart—and this was driving her crazy—was excitedly bouncing around at the thought of having Blake staying with her.

It was a ridiculous idea. Adamantly, she shook her head. "I don't need any looking after, thank you very much. And even if… Please note the 'if'…you stay at the house, there is no reason to pretend we're a couple. This is the twenty-first century."

Opening the car door, she jumped out. "I could stay with Eleanor or Brooke. I'm not lying to anyone. Besides, nobody will believe we're a couple. I don't even like you."

He got out quickly and put his hand out to stop her from leaving. "If you stay with other people, you'll be putting them in danger, as well. Just think about it. You don't have to like me, but I am going to stay with you until this guy is behind bars, even if I stay out on the porch."

Shrugging off his arm, she stomped towards the entrance of the bar. After a few steps, she turned around, her eyes narrowing. "How do you know Logan and Charlie are in Seattle and Gavin is in South Africa? Do you keep tabs on my family? But the biggest question is why do you know all these things about my life?"

"Let's have dinner. Maybe you'll be in a better mood once you've eaten." And while she was still sputtering, he put a hand behind her back and guided her towards the entrance of the bar.

Under his hand, her whole body was shaking. Blake clenched his teeth. None of the questions she'd just asked weren't ones he hadn't asked himself a few hundred times over the past week.

The simple answer was he was worried about her because there seemed to be someone out there, intent on harming her. He'd always protected and served—that had been his job—it was also the way he lived his life.

But the answer to why he felt so protective towards Lindsay Wilson wasn't one he wanted to think about for too long. The mere thought something could happen to her made him break out in a cold sweat.

So no, there weren't any logical answers to any of her questions, but he had to do this. It was that simple.

ELSA WINCKLER

CHAPTER 2

Shaking, Lindsay stumbled, and a big hand caught her arm and held it tightly. It would be so easy to rely on Blake for support and help, but she'd been struggling to rebuild her life after Mark Taylor had nearly destroyed her self-confidence and sense of worth. She'd finally found peace, a place she could call home, she was doing a job she loved, and there were people in her life she could call friends.

But first, she'd received a message from freaking Mark telling her he was coming for her, and then Blake had showed up, making her feel things she didn't want to feel.

Before he could steer her into the bar, she pulled her arm out of his hold, turned, and walked back towards the street. She felt like crying and had to get home before she fell apart.

Why did the mere mention of Mark's name still freak her out? For too long she'd given him the power to systematically break down her self-confidence and make her doubt her every decision.

She'd met him right after her parents' accident, at a point when her whole life had been shattered. Of course, afterwards, it had been easy to see why she'd allowed him to just about take over her life. She'd been desperately looking for a home and family to replace the one she'd lost. At the time, Charlie was also in and out of hospital with the injury she'd sustained during the same accident, and without her sister, Lindsay had been so lost.

Initially, she'd thought she'd found another safe haven with Mark. She'd thought the way he'd nearly suffocated her with attention was because he was caring. Even when he'd gradually begun to cut her off from her friends and sister, she'd seen it as concern about her well-being.

It had taken more than a few months, but she'd discovered the only person he ever really cared about was himself. Things quickly spiraled out of control, up to a point where she hadn't felt safe around his mood swings anymore. And on the night he'd furiously raised his hand and forbade her to see her sister Charlie again, she knew it was time to break things off.

Only it hadn't been that easy. He'd hounded her for days with messages and emails until she'd changed all her numbers and her email addresses. Fortunately, at the same time, Charlie had inherited their Aunt Charlene's house and a building here in Alisson, Montana, and they could cross an ocean, moving far away from South Africa.

They both had fond memories of the town where they'd spent many Christmases with their mom and dad and Aunt Charlene. Neither she nor Charlie had anyone keeping them in South Africa except Gavin, their brother, so deciding to move here was an easy decision to make. Fortunately, after Gavin's visit to them earlier this year, he'd also decided to relocate to Alisson.

She and Charlie had been very careful and didn't leave any forwarding addresses to anyone but their brother. But then Gavin's emails had been hacked and someone started following her, and she had to face the fact that Mark had been looking for her. And he'd found her.

And now on top of that, Blake was stirring feelings inside her she knew she couldn't trust, and the dream she'd had of creating a simple life for herself was turning into a nightmare.

"Damn it, Lindsay, where are you going?" Blake was right behind her.

"Home," she said, and continued walking. "Go away. I can look after myself." She was nearing the street and walked faster, quickly looking up and down to see if any vehicles were coming her way. One car was coming down the street, but it was moving so slowly, she should make it across before it reached this spot. She took a step down from the pavement.

"Lindsay—look out!" Blake called out behind her.

As if in slow motion, she turned her head to see a car, a green one, she registered, driving straight at her. Mesmerized, unable to move, she stared at the approaching lights. Behind her, more voices cried out and then a pair of strong arms lifted her away just before the car would've hit her.

Blake's arms gathered her close. Shuddering, she buried her face in his neck. She'd so nearly been hit by that car. If Blake hadn't been here…

"What happened?" Lindsay recognized Eleanor's voice.

Oh, damn, she shouldn't be in Blake's arms when Eleanor was around. Within seconds, the older woman would jump to all sorts of conclusions.

Inhaling, Lindsay quickly moved away from Blake, and he dropped his arms. Eleanor and her daughter, Brooke, rushed closer. Lindsay wished the earth could open up and swallow her whole. Her heart was still pumping out of control after the surge of adrenaline, and now she had to face an additional problem.

The last thing she needed at this point was for Eleanor to try her matchmaking skills on her. Eleanor was the mother of Charlie's new husband Logan, and both she and Brooke had been so helpful when she and Charlie had first arrived in Allison. But Eleanor, bless her meddling heart, was a die-hard romantic, always looking for the next love story in town. And if there weren't any, she would conjure up imagined relationships and do her best to "help" whichever couple she thought needed her "support."

"Another car tried to run her down just now," Blake said brusquely, looking over his shoulder towards the street.

"What car?" Brooke asked.

"One I noticed earlier. I should've…" And cursing under his breath, he put a hand on Lindsay's shoulder. "I need to make a phone call and then I'll take you home."

"What can we do?" asked Eleanor.

"We haven't eaten. We were on our way to dinner—" Blake began.

"Don't worry, we'll bring Lindsay something to eat," Brooke interrupted. "What about you?"

"I'll be staying with her for the time being, so yes, something for me, too, thanks." And while Eleanor stared at him open-mouthed, he took out his wallet and gave it to Brooke.

Once more, Lindsay wished the earth would open up. Gathering her wits, she lifted her chin. "Seriously, Blake…" she began hotly.

But Eleanor had finally found her voice again. She clapped her hands. "What is going on here? Brooke, can you feel the sparks? Please tell me the two of you are together? What did I tell you, Brooke? They were absolutely made for each other. I swear, I can literally feel the vibes around the two of you whenever you're—"

"No!" Lindsay called out, frantic to stop Eleanor's excitement. "We're…we're not a couple. There is absolutely nothing going on between us, and there is certainly no need for Blake to stay with me."

Eleanor's eyebrows rose as her gaze flitted between Blake and Lindsay. "If you say so, my dear. I'm just calling it as I see it." She grinned. "You two together are just pure magic."

"Mark Taylor caught a flight to Bozeman and he arrived in Montana yesterday," Blake said, wiping the smile from Eleanor's face.

Eleanor and Brooke exclaimed in horror, but Lindsay tuned out. The bright lights of the green car coming towards her flashed in front of eyes again. Earlier that year, after she'd received the initial threatening email from Mark, there had been a similar incident where a car had tried to run her down, and Charlie had been injured—the incident Blake had referred to earlier.

After she'd told Mark it was over between them, he'd warned her he wasn't letting her go so easily but never in her wildest dreams did she think he would stoop to trying to hurt her, or something even worse. She bit her lip. It hadn't been something she'd wanted to believe, but after two similar incidents, it was becoming clear he was even more of a threat to her than she'd thought. Charlie had been hurt in the first incident and just now, if it hadn't been for Blake... She shuddered.

"Well, anyway, I think it would be a wonderful idea if Blake can stay with you while Charlie and Logan are in Seattle and Gavin has left for South Africa," Eleanor continued. "Charlie was so worried about leaving you here on your own, and Gavin phones daily to find out whether you're still okay. It'll be such a comfort to them to know that Blake is back and that he'll be staying with you. It really is such a relief, sweetie; I can't tell you how worried we've all been."

Lindsay had opened her mouth to state again that she'd been living on her own for quite some time now, but she swallowed her words. The last thing she wanted was for Charlie and Gavin to worry about her.

Charlie had married the love of her life in September and was so obviously happy, Lindsay didn't want her to have to return earlier to Alisson because of her. And Gavin, their brother who'd been living in South Africa, had flown out to see them after Lindsay had received the first message from Mark. Since then, he'd decided he was going to also relocate to Alisson, but he'd needed a few months to settle his affairs in South Africa. And she knew if he thought she was in danger, he'd catch the next plane to Bozeman.

So she was more or less forced to let Blake stay with her. It would reassure both Charlie and Gavin to know someone they knew was staying with Lindsay. In theory, it made sense.

The reality of sharing a house with the seriously sexy Blake, though, was something completely different. Every time she came near him, her hormones went ballistic.

"Okay, then it's settled," Blake was saying. "We'll swing by my place to pick up a bag and then I'll take Lindsay home—"

"No need, I can go with Eleanor and Brooke," Lindsay interrupted. She desperately needed a few minutes away from his brooding and unsettling presence.

"I'd prefer…" Blake began, but Lindsay smiled and caught Brooke's arm.

She lifted her chin. "If you are going to be around me, you'll have to learn you're not always going to get your way."

Again, something flashed in his eyes, but without saying anything else, he turned around, and taking his phone out, continued to walk towards his car.

Eleanor waved a hand in front of herself. "Wow, sweetie, I know you've said there isn't anything between the two of you, but those hot vibes going around are threatening to scorch everyone in sight!"

"No vibes, Eleanor, just irritation. For some reason or another, he feels he has to protect me, but neither of us is very pleased about the idea."

"Well, my dear"—Eleanor grinned—"it's nearly Christmas. You never know. There's magic in the air, haven't you noticed? So come on, let's go and order something to eat while we wait."

"How are you feeling, Lindsay?" Brooke asked. "You're still very pale. Don't you think we should phone the doctor?"

"I'm totally fine, thanks, Brooke. Just hungry," Lindsay said, but she caught the look between Eleanor and her daughter. She wasn't fooling anyone, it seemed.

Half an hour later, Blake parked his car next to Lindsay's house. He got out and walked back towards the street. It was quiet. Some owners had already put up Christmas decorations, he noticed, as he looked up and down the rows of houses. All were brightly lit, the streetlights were on; things seemed perfectly ordinary.

But he was on edge. Someone was lurking around, intent on harming Lindsay. The attacks were escalating, something that was freaking him out. Whoever had been behind the wheel of the green car was clearly out of control. His gut was telling him it was probably Taylor. And the mere thought that someone could hurt her made him want to break things.

She was so fragile at the moment. He grimaced. Not something he'd mention in front of her, though. He could already imagine those blue eyes shooting darts in his direction.

With a last glance down the street, he walked back to his car and took out his bag. Eleanor's car was still in front of the house, he was glad to see. He didn't want Lindsay to be alone for any length of time.

When he'd received the call a few days before from an informant he'd been paying to keep an eye on Mark Taylor's movements, he'd caught the first flight from Reagan Airport in Washington, DC.

Taylor was on his way to Alisson, he was told. Fortunately, the case he'd been helping the FBI with had been solved, and the agent-in-charge had given him the go-ahead to return to Alisson. His former employers had wanted him to stay and help them with another ongoing investigation into an elusive gang of bank robbers, and he'd promised to join them later, when he could. But first he had to make sure Lindsay was safe. For the moment, she was his priority.

Ever since he'd first seen her that first night in the bar, his protective instincts had kicked in, and that had been before he knew about the threatening message from her ex. There was a haunted look in her eyes and a wariness in her movements that was urging him on—against his better judgment—to safeguard her.

Why he was here was something he didn't want to think about too much. What he did know was that he was nobody's damn hero—the very dead body of his last partner, Will Miller, had made that abundantly clear.

The front door opened and the porchlight was switched on. Lindsay walked out. "Oh, it's you," she said, and crossed her arms. "We heard something but when nobody knocked, we weren't sure it was you."

With two steps he was at her side and touched her arm. "I didn't mean to frighten you, sorry. I went to check the street again."

Troubled blue eyes looked up at him, and it was all he could do not to take her in his arms and tell her everything would be all right. It wasn't a promise he'd ever make again. But his hand was touching her face before his brain got the message doing so would be a very bad idea.

For a millisecond, she stared at him before she turned away. "Please lock the door—we're in the dining room."

He locked the door, took a step forward, and stilled. For the first time, the implication of his rash announcement dawned on him. He was going to stay here. With Lindsay. Her sister wasn't here, her brother wasn't here. It would only be the two of them alone in this house.

Exhaling slowly, he continued after Lindsay. When he'd suggested he'd stay with her, his only thought had been to make sure nothing happened to her; he hadn't thought it through.

Damn it to hell. *Focus, Davidson, focus.* He was here to

protect her. That was it. And maybe if he repeated that a few hundred times, he'd remember why he shouldn't notice the softness of her hair, the way her mouth curled up when she smiled, and he wouldn't remember the perfect way she fitted against his body.

As he entered the dining room, Lindsay bent down to pick up something from the floor, and he nearly groaned out loud. Her jeans dipped, revealing a glimpse of black lace.

All the blood left his head and pooled way below his middle. Damn, she was killing him without even knowing it. Gulping in fresh air, he forced himself to look away. Who the hell was he kidding? Protecting Lindsay was way different to any other job he'd ever done.

For starters, no other body he'd ever been assigned to protect had affected him this much.

He met Eleanor's twinkling eyes. "Come and sit down, Blake," she called out, and motioned to an empty chair.

Brooke handed him his wallet. "We haven't used all your money, don't worry," she joked.

He put his wallet back in the pocket of his pants. "Thanks for bringing Lindsay home. I don't want her left alone before we catch this guy."

CHAPTER 3

Fuming, Lindsay opened the cupboard to take out another glass and plate. She was still recovering from the incident earlier and had been hoping against hope Blake would realize how utterly ridiculous his idea to stay with her was.

But here he was, with luggage, making it clear he was going to sleep here. The kitchen, dining room, and living room were one big, open area, but the moment Blake had entered the room, the place seemed to have shrunk.

She was acutely aware of his every movement. The subtle tones of sandalwood and nutmeg that always surrounded him had seeped into her pores, making it impossible to smell anything else, even the delicious food Brooke had bought.

As she handed him his glass, Eleanor leaned forward. "So Blake, do tell us where you've been over the past few months. You made a quick appearance at Charlie and Logan's wedding, but then you disappeared again. And call me inquisitive, but how on earth did you know Lindsay's ex was on his way here?"

With his eyes on his glass, Blake nodded. Lindsay sat down on the chair next to him. These were all questions she was dying to ask but didn't dare.

"I still do work for a previous employer on a consulting basis. So…" He turned to look at Lindsay, "When I heard about your ex—"

"Mark," she interrupted. "Please don't call him 'my' anything."

"Let's just say, I have contacts," he finished.

Eleanor's eyes widened. "So who did you work for? FBI? CIA? KFC? Oh, no, sorry, that's chicken." She grinned.

"Mom, seriously." Brooke laughed, interrupting her mother. She got up. "Come on, let me get you home before you start asking Blake about his family tree."

Blake grimaced and also stood up. "That's easy. I don't have one. Grew up in the system. Let me walk you outside."

His jaw tightened, his eyes darkened, and for a moment, Lindsay had the urge to put her arms around him. There was obviously more to his story than he was prepared to tell.

"Please let us know if we can do anything else," Brooke was saying.

Both Brooke and Eleanor had picked up their handbags and were on their way to leave. Suddenly panicking, Lindsay grabbed Brooke's hand. "Surely you can stay a little bit longer. There's still so much food left."

But Eleanor smiled and patted her hand. "We'll be at the bar tomorrow night—we'll see you then?"

Lindsay nodded, her mouth suddenly dry. Within seconds, Brooke and Eleanor would be gone and she'd be left alone with Blake Davidson. Just the two of them.

Help.

"You haven't eaten anything yet," Lindsay said, and pointed towards the food on the table. They were still standing after they'd both been out to see Eleanor and

Brooke off. She was nervous. On edge.

"Have you eaten?" Blake asked. Maybe if they did something ordinary, like eating, the heat he could literally feel building up between them would diminish.

She shook her head and crossed her arms. "Being nearly hit by a car kinda robbed me of my appetite."

"I'm here to make sure that won't happen again. Glass of wine?"

She hesitated but then pulled out a chair. "Thanks. I'm not sure whether the food isn't cold by now…"

He poured the wine and put a glass in front of her before he also sat down opposite her. "It'll be fine."

For a few minutes she sipped on her wine while he helped himself to the lasagna Brooke had bought.

"I really don't think you have to stay here," she finally said.

He didn't answer but continued eating. He wasn't wasting words on a conversation they'd already had.

"I'll make sure the doors are locked. It doesn't make any sense for you to also be here."

He continued eating.

"Blake, damn it—you have to say something!"

"Eat."

Muttering, she dished some of the lasagna into her plate. "I'm a big girl…"

He looked up; blue eyes met his. "Oh, I've noticed."

She inhaled sharply. "That's not…I don't… You make me so mad!"

"Eat."

He finished his plate before he leaned back in the chair. Her eyes were on him, wary, questioning, and filled with another emotion he couldn't quite figure out.

She didn't eat much and after a few bites, she pushed her plate away. "I've eaten. Now talk."

"There is an obvious disturbed individual hell-bent on getting to you, one way or another. Both your sister and brother are away at the moment. So I'm here to make sure that doesn't happen."

"What about the police or the sheriff's department?"

"I can be here at night. In the same house."

She glared at him. "I don't like it."

He had no answer to that. She got up and began clearing the table. He helped and within minutes, they'd cleaned the kitchen. He was trying his best to ignore the flowery scent surrounding her, the way she was chewing her lower lip, and her soft curls that touched him whenever he got too close to her.

"I'm going to bed," she finally said. "Let me show you where you can sleep."

"I'm happy to use the couch."

"Not necessary. I've moved into Charlie's old room. Gavin's room is full of his stuff, but I cleared out my old room when I moved to Charlie's. The bed is made up."

Grabbing his bag, he followed her up the stairs, forcing his eyes to stay on her feet while one thought kept going round and round in his head. He'd be sleeping in her bed. Damn.

And she'd be close by. Oh, man. Clenching his jaw, he counted the stairs until they finally reached the second level of the house. After she was in bed, he would come down again to check that everything was locked.

Lindsay walked to the first door and opened it. "The room has its own bathroom. Let me know if you need anything. There should be clean towels…"

She turned; he'd stepped forward; they met up real close.

"Thank you," he said, his eyes on her soft lips. This close, her scent reeled him in. Quickly, he put his hand not holding the bag into his pocket.

"Good night," she said, chewing her lip.

Damn, she was killing him. He nodded and waited for her to leave. But she didn't.

For long moments they stared at one another. It would be the easiest thing to bring her closer, to kiss her. To pull that soft, lacy top over her head and to…

"You should go to your room," he got out.

She didn't immediately move.

With a groan, he put out his hand and touched her lips. "Otherwise, I'm going to kiss you. It's all I can think of."

This time, she fled.

He had to lean against the door frame for a moment as he watched her entering the room next to his. How the hell was he supposed to sleep, knowing she was on the other side of a thin wall?

Cursing a blue streak, he walked into the room and closed the door behind him. He was here to protect her. That was it.

The last time he hadn't been focused on what he was supposed to be doing, someone got killed.

There were still a million butterflies going crazy in her tummy by the time Lindsay switched off her bedside light. She'd tried to read. When that hadn't worked, she'd tried mindful meditation. After she'd broken it off with Mark, this technique had helped her feel whole again. And usually, when focusing on her breathing, keeping other thoughts at bay, she could relax.

But the thought of Blake Davidson's eyes on her mouth simply refused to be kept at bay, or pushed to any other place than firmly in her mind.

Finally, she added two drops of lavender, eucalyptus, and peppermint in the diffuser she kept in her room. Hopefully, the relaxing aromas would help her to fall asleep. While Blake Davidson was sleeping in her old room. Only a short few steps from where she was lying.

Otherwise, I'm going to kiss you. It's all I can think of. His words had lit a fire inside her, one that was still smoldering just below the surface.

She hadn't thought she'd ever be interested in a man again, but one look from Blake all those months ago, and she'd realized whatever she'd felt for Mark paled in comparison to the overwhelming feelings she experienced when he'd first laid those chocolate brown eyes on her.

There. She'd admitted it. He annoyed her, he irritated her, but every single one of her senses responded to him.

Groaning out loud, she pulled the blanket over her head like she used to do when she was small and she wanted bad things to disappear.

It could all be explained: she hadn't been with anyone in a long time, Blake was devastatingly attractive, and on top of that, she was on edge because she'd nearly been run over by a car again. Probably also Mark's doing. No wonder her hormones and dopamine levels were out of control.

The sound of glass breaking downstairs brought her quickly back to reality. With her heart racing, she threw the blankets off, jumped out of bed, and ran towards her door. There was another sound. Swallowing down her fear, she opened the door. The light in the corridor was on.

"Blake?" she called out, and moved towards his room. But the door to his room was open and he wasn't inside.

She turned and rushed down the stairs. "Blake?" she called out again and stormed into the kitchen. He was standing over broken glass on the ground, shirtless, his phone against his ear. Her eyes zoomed in on his tanned, muscled six-pack. Oh, my.

"Don't move!" Blake's voice was urgent, but she'd already put her foot down.

"Ouch!" she called out and with one stride Blake had put his phone down and was beside her. Cursing under his breath, he picked her up. "Why the hell don't you ever listen?" he growled.

Her hands landed on his naked torso and she quickly pulled them back. "I didn't do anything wrong, don't scold me! Why is there broken glass on the floor?"

He placed her on the kitchen counter and lifted her foot. "Your foot is bleeding. Band-Aid?"

"I can get it…"

"There are pieces of glass all over the floor. And you'll bleed all over the place."

"Seriously, Blake…"

"And ointment?"

Fed up with him, the stupid butterflies in her tummy, and her out-of-control hormones, she pointed to the medicine cupboard while she turned her foot to see what was going on.

She'd stepped on a miniscule piece of glass. "This is such a tiny piece of glass, I really don't need ointment. Just a Band-Aid to stop the bleeding." She pulled out the piece of glass as he approached with a Band-Aid and ointment in hand. "Give it to me. I assure you I can put a Band-Aid on my own foot; I'm a trained nurse."

But he brushed her hand aside. "I'll do it." Bending his head, he proceeded to clean the wound. He'd showered, his hair was still wet. The scent of soap and man were playing havoc with her hormones, the butterflies in her tummy going wild.

"There you go," he said gruffly and looked up. Brown eyes darkened; around the two of them, the air thickened.

She held her breath. If she moved an inch, she knew, she'd unleash something potent and exciting. Question was, was she ready for potent and exciting?

He stepped back; the moment passed. "Broom?" he asked.

She pointed towards another cupboard, looking away quickly. He did have swoon-worthy muscled shoulders and a killer backside, but she really didn't have to actually swoon about it.

For the first time, she looked at the glass on the floor. She swept her gaze up to the window and inhaled sharply. "The window is broken…" she whispered.

Blake didn't answer immediately but swiped all the pieces together.

"Blake? What happened to the window?"

He pointed towards a piece of rock sitting on the kitchen counter she hadn't noticed before. "This was thrown through the window."

She could literally feel the blood leaving her face. "Mark," she whispered. "It has to be him. So he managed to get close to me…"

Before she could finish her sentence, the sound of a vehicle stopping right outside froze the words in her throat. It couldn't be Mark? Could it?

Blake didn't look at her but moved towards the door. "It's the police. Go up to your room. I'll deal with them."

She slid down the kitchen counter. "It's my house." Ignoring him, she gave a step towards the front door. But the next minute, he'd picked her up again.

"Damn it, Blake…" she ranted as he rushed up the stairs with her in his arms.

"Get dressed," he growled as he put her down in front of her room. "You're not wearing a bra. I damn well don't want any other man to see you like this."

Before her brain had time to reassemble and make sense of what was happening, he'd put her down and was marching towards his own room. She was still standing where he'd left her when seconds later, he came out of his room again, buttoning up a shirt.

Just then, the doorbell chimed. With one heated look in her direction, he jogged down the stairs.

What was his problem, damn it? She was wearing a pair of perfectly respectable, very un-sexy, flannel pajamas. What was he going on about? Annoyed, she glanced down and gulped. The top two buttons had become undone, giving anyone around her a clear view of her boobs.

Blake's heated gaze… Oh, my goodness.

Blake closed the front door and leaned against it for a moment. The police van would stay close by for the night.

The broken window had to be secured in some way

until morning, when he'd be able to replace the glass. The local hardware store should have everything he needed to do that.

He glanced up the stairs before he entered the kitchen. Lindsay hadn't appeared while the police were here. Hopefully, she'd be in bed.

In the kitchen he came to an abrupt halt. Crouching in front of the window, hammer in hand, was Lindsay.

"What the hell are you doing?" He reached her in two strides.

She hammered another nail into a piece of wood the size of the broken windowpane before she stood up. "Securing the window the best way I know how until the shops open tomorrow."

"Damn it, Lindsay, that's something I can do…"

"Why? I can use a hammer. My dad showed Charlie and me how to do basic things with a hammer when we were still at school."

She'd put on another top over her pajama top, probably thinking that it hid the fact she still wasn't wearing a bra. But her generous breasts were swaying freely as she moved, making it clear she hadn't listened to him. Trying to conceal the way his body was reacting to her, he crouched down to check the window. It was good enough for the time being.

"You should think about installing a security system or at least have burglar bars put in for the downstairs windows," he said.

"Nobody in Alisson has burglar bars," she muttered, gathering the hammer and nails lying around.

"Nobody in Alisson has a psycho ex-boyfriend intent on hurting them."

With jerky movements, she turned away and put the hammer and nails in a drawer. Ignoring him, she left the kitchen.

Swearing, he closed the blinds and switched off the lights. He probably shouldn't have said that about her ex.

But damn it, after everything that had happened, she was still hell-bent on doing things her way.

He stopped in front of his room. The door to her room was closed. Slowly, he moved towards it. It was quiet inside; she was probably in bed already.

But as he turned away, he heard the sound. She was crying. Fisting his hands, he quickly walked back to his room and closed the door behind him. His whole being was urging him to go inside her room, pick her up, and comfort her—the reason why he had to stay as far away from her as possible. Because if he were to touch her again…

Cursing, he switched off the light and glanced out the window. The police van was parked outside. For the time being, at least, Lindsay was safe.

He pressed his ear against the wall and stood like that until the crying stopped.

CHAPTER 4

Saturday morning, early, Lindsay was up and dressed. Last night's crying had been a good thing; most of her pent-up anger and panic had been released.

But now she had to get out of the house as soon as possible. Her shop was open on Saturday mornings, and Saturday afternoons she usually spent mixing oils and making sure she had enough stock in the shop for the week ahead. Over the past week she'd received quite a few requests from clients who wanted various blends of oils for all sorts of ailments, ranging from headaches to snoring husbands, so she had more than enough to do to keep her busy all afternoon.

She and Charlie had converted the building Charlie had inherited from their Aunt Charlene into two parts. One the one side, Charlie had her rooms where she saw her clients for Bowden treatments, and Lindsay had turned the other side into her shop. At the back, attached to her shop, was a smaller room she used as a studio, where she mixed her essential oils and skincare products.

They were both healers—her dad used to tease them. Ever since they were small, they'd bring home stray and hurt animals, to their mother's dismay. So it hadn't come as any surprise when they'd both taken up nursing after school. And now they'd both found their own unique way of healing and helping people. Charlie had her Bowden Therapy and she had discovered the healing power of essential oils.

Her phone rang. Great, it was Stacy Lawrence. There weren't many young people in Alisson, and when she'd met Stacy, during one of Blake's self-defense classes at his dojo, they'd immediately clicked.

Stacy was also originally from South Africa and had moved to Alisson recently. Exactly what her story was, wasn't clear. Stacey never gave a direct answer to anyone's queries about her past, something that was driving Eleanor crazy. They all liked her, though, and were very glad about the small printing shop she'd opened. On top of that, she was also a computer whiz, and among the many things she could do, she designed websites—the reason why Lindsay had contacted her a while ago.

"Hi, Lindsay," Stacy greeted her. "Sorry I'm only now phoning you, but it's been a crazy week. Are you in the shop today? I can come and see you anytime."

"Great. Whenever suits you." They organized a time before Stacy rang off.

Smiling for the first time since she'd opened her eyes, Lindsay put her phone away. She'd been thinking about the idea of selling her products online, and the first step would be to get her own website. Up until now, she'd been reluctant to share any information about herself online because she'd been worried Mark would try and find her. But now that he'd tracked her down anyway, it didn't really matter anymore. An online presence would give her a wider network of clients.

Just thinking of Mark made her shiver.

She hated feeling on edge all the time. Why couldn't the police or the sheriff catch him?

Slowly, she walked down the stairs. In the cold light of day, the events of the previous evening seemed surreal.

But the sounds coming from the kitchen were very real, emphasizing the fact she wasn't alone in this house because Mark was threatening her safety.

And now Blake was here, living with her, under the same roof. Sleeping in the room next to hers. And immediately those stupid butterflies were back. She pressed her hand to her tummy. Seriously. The only reason he was here, at all, was because of her "psycho ex-boyfriend," as he'd called Mark. Pressing her lips together, she stepped into the kitchen.

Blake was in front of the stove and didn't turn around to look at her. "Morning. I've made coffee. Pancakes coming up."

"You cook?"

"I like to eat; therefore, I've taught myself to cook."

Not a man of many words. She poured coffee into a mug, and leaning against the kitchen counter, looked at him. Muscles rippled underneath the lightweight white sweater he was wearing.

She tried to inhale, but for some or other strange reason, she was finding it difficult to get enough oxygen in her lungs. Oh, my goodness, this was ridiculous.

"I'm sorry about my remark last night about your...about Taylor." Blake still didn't turn around to face her.

Just then, her phone rang. Relieved to be doing something other than staring at Blake, she checked her phone. It was Charlie.

Oh, damn, her sister had probably heard about the car that had nearly run her over. She kept forgetting everyone knew everyone's business in the small town of Alisson, Montana. Except Stacey's, of course. She'd been hoping it wouldn't be necessary to tell Charlie that Blake was staying here. But she should have known Charlie would hear about it sooner or later, if not from Eleanor or Brooke, then from someone else.

"Hi, Charlie—" But that was as far as she got.

"Mark Taylor is back in Allison and you didn't let me know?" Charlie cried out. "I had to learn that from Eleanor when she has just phoned to say she and Brooke wanted to join us here in Seattle for a few days. We're on our way back, of course; we're not staying here when—"

"No, please don't. I'm absolutely fine—"

"How can you say that? He tried to run you over again last night!"

"I know, but..."

"I can't stay here and know you're in danger, Linds. I'll never sleep. We'll try to catch the next—"

"You'll do no such thing!" Lindsay interrupted her. "Blake is staying here. Until the police can catch Mark."

For a few moments, the line was quiet.

"Charlie? Are you still there?"

"Yes, I'm still here," Charlie finally said. "I'm just not sure I've heard you correctly. Blake as in Blake Davidson? Your self-defense instructor? The same Blake who was one of Logan's groomsmen? Blake Davison, the guy you don't like, is staying with you?"

Before Lindsay could answer, Blake had taken the phone from her. "Yes, Charlie, it's Blake. And yes, I'm staying with Lindsay until Taylor is caught." His eyes were on Lindsay. "Even if your sister doesn't like me." And with that, he handed back her phone.

Lindsay turned away. Nobody had invited the damn man into their conversation. "It's just temporary," she said to Charlie.

"Well, I can't tell you how relieved I am to hear you're not alone. Logan would've dropped everything he still had to do, but now I know Blake is staying there, we don't have to rush back, and Logan can finalize all his business before we return. And also, Eleanor and Brooke can come and visit, too. Are you okay about it, though? I know he's not your favorite person."

"I'll be fine, don't worry about me. Tell me how you're feeling? Baby still okay?"

A sure way to get her sister to talk about something else was to talk about her pregnancy. There was a time Charlie thought she'd never be able to have children.

They talked for a few minutes longer before Charlie ended the call. Lindsay stared at her phone, an idea taking shape in her mind. What if she joined Eleanor and Brooke when they visited Logan and Charlie in Seattle? That way, she could get away from Alisson until they'd caught Mark. She'd also escape Blake's constant presence, and an additional bonus would be she could see her suppliers in Seattle.

Relieved to have some sort of plan, she put her phone down and finished her coffee.

"Come and have something to eat," Blake said, and put a plate full of pancakes on the table.

Her mouth watered and she pulled out a chair. "I love the American version of pancakes."

"I didn't know there were other versions," Blake said.

"In South Africa, we call what you've made crumpets or flapjacks, but for us a pancake is bigger and flatter and we eat it rolled up, with cinnamon sugar. But I love these, too."

Blake sat down and they began to eat.

"Everything okay?" he asked.

She nodded, her mouth already full of syrupy pancakes.

For a few minutes it was silent. She kept her eyes on her pancakes but she was aware of his eyes on her.

Finally, he cleared his throat. "I keep hearing you don't like me. Any particular reason?"

"You're always frowning when you look at me."

But he wasn't listening to her any longer. His eyes were on her mouth. Again. Her breath hitched in her throat. The next moment, he reached across the table and wiped the corner of her mouth with his thumb.

As if in a trance, her eyes followed his thumb back to his mouth where his tongue shot out and licked it. Oh, my. She felt that lick right down to her very core.

"You had some syrup on your lip." His voice was gruff, sending shivers down her spine. "And just for the record, I like you. Way too much for my piece of mind. I told you I want to kiss you."

Stunned, she stared at him until a car started up nearby. Rattled, she jumped up. The last thing she wanted to be reminded of was the way she'd hovered in his room the night before. He had to mention kissing her before she'd fled. "I'll be in the shop all day." She was a little out of breath, but hopefully, Blake wouldn't notice.

"Will you be alone?" Blake asked.

"Lilly will be there," Lindsay said quickly while she cleared the table. He didn't have to know Lilly left at noon on Saturdays. Nothing could happen to her while she was in her shop. On either side of their building were other businesses; there were other people around. But she needed to get away from Blake before she did something really stupid.

She was nervous and on edge—that was the only reason she was reacting to Blake's presence like a lovesick schoolgirl.

"I'm going to check in on the dojo before I get the necessary items to repair the window," Blake said.

Lindsay looked up quickly. Oh, my goodness, she'd completely forgotten about the broken window. Seriously? Having Blake so close was really messing with her brain.

"You don't have to do that. I should be able to slip out during the morning to buy what is needed."

Warily, she glanced at him. Taking a stand about anything was still a novelty to her. Mark's erratic behavior had taught her to keep quiet and agree with his suggestions. But this wasn't Mark and she wasn't the same person she'd been two years ago.

The muscle in his jaw moved a few times. "I know you're perfectly capable of doing it yourself. But I need to do something. Let me do this, please?"

She sighed. It would be better if he got whatever was

needed; Saturday mornings were usually quite busy. And he did ask nicely.

Nodding, she poured more syrup on the pancake. "Let me know what I owe you."

He looked at her but didn't answer.

"A friend, Jason Coleman, has been helping out at the dojo," he said after a few minutes. "He tells me you haven't been back for your self-defense classes since I've left?"

She shrugged. "Yes, I know about him. Charlie got married. We were busy."

"Charlie is now married. And I'm back."

"I'll think about it."

The beginnings of a smile turned up the corners of his mouth ever so slightly. "Let me know when you're ready to leave. I'll drop you off at work and I'll pick you up whatever time you've finished."

"I can drive myself to work, seriously…"

He caught her hand. "I don't want to fight with you. Please?"

Warm, brown eyes stared down at her. The butterflies loved this and went mad. Irritated, she pulled her hand out of his and turned away. "Do those chocolate brown eyes always work for you?" The minute the words left her mouth she wished she could make them disappear into thin air.

A low chuckle came from behind her. "Chocolate?"

Muttering, she stomped away. Staying in the same house with Blake Davidson was so not working out for her. She'd speak to Brooke as soon as possible about joining them when they went to Seattle.

Over the last two years, she'd worked hard to create a calm and quiet life for herself. After her parents' sudden death, Charlie's injury, and on top of that, the whole bad experience she'd had with Mark, she'd rebuilt her life step by step, with her sister's help, of course.

But now Charlie was married and she didn't want to

rely on her sister any longer. Mark had been her mistake, no one else's, and she would have to sort out this mess.

She'd never been one for crowds and noise; she needed peace and silence around her ever since she could remember. But now that the lovely people in Alisson had become aware of the fact that Mark was trying to hurt her, she'd been overwhelmed by everyone's concern. Truth be told, she hated being the center of attention.

And it would be so easy to become dependent on others to fix her problems again but she wouldn't allow it. Her mistakes—she had to find the solutions.

Her life was anything but peaceful at the moment and she hated that. And okay, yes, maybe everyone, including Blake, thought he was helping her but in fact he was adding to her agitation.

Pressing a hand against her tummy, she raced up the stairs. These stupid butterflies had only appeared when she'd first met him. He was stirring something inside of her, and even though her instincts were telling her he was a completely different man to Mark Taylor, she wasn't sure she could trust her own feelings again.

Even before his car had come to a complete standstill, Lindsay had opened her door.

"Thank you. I…I'll get home by myself…"

Muttering under his breath, he got out and followed Lindsay to the entrance of her workplace. The woman was driving him crazy. It was cold, she was wrapped up in a coat, and a scarf and a beanie covered her hair, but he'd seen the soft, blue lace top hugging her breasts in the kitchen, and he couldn't get the damn picture out of his head.

While she unlocked the door, he turned and looked up and down the street. All around them, businesses were opening, people were walking, cars were driving up and down the street. Across the street was a coffee shop and through the window he could see several customers enjoying their breakfast.

The uneasiness from yesterday was back. He'd always relied on his gut and it was telling him something was off. He just couldn't put his finger on it. Once Lindsay was behind the counter, he'd stroll over to see if any strangers were lurking around.

"I'm fine now," Lindsay was saying, but he ignored her and stepped in front of her to enter first.

"Wait here," he said, scanning the small interior as he walked around.

"What are you doing?" she asked, clearly irritated.

He didn't answer but walked towards the section of the building where Charlie's rooms were.

"Blake, seriously, what are you doing? There are people outside. Nobody…"

He turned around quickly; she was right behind him. Her hands landed on his arms. Blue eyes darkened. Desire. That was the emotion he'd seen before and couldn't identify. But now, this close, he recognized the familiar emotion.

"Damn, Lindsay…" He barely got the words out, then slipped his hands around her neck.

"Halloo!" a voice called out.

Lindsay put her hands on his arms and pushed them down. "I…I have to go. It's Lilly." She turned away.

"I'll be there in a minute."

"You can really go now, I'll be fine."

"In a minute," he said through clenched teeth.

"But why…?" she began, turning back to face him, a frown on her face.

Cursing, he pulled her close, making sure she felt what she was doing to him.

Her eyes widened and she stilled. "Oh."

"Yeah. *Oh.* I need a minute."

He'd thought she'd be angry. He'd reckoned she'd move away quickly. Counted on it, truth be told. But she didn't move. And his body, clearly very happy with her closeness, reacted with speed to her nearness.

"Lindsay? Anybody here?" Lilly called again.

Only then Lindsay turned around. "I'm here. Coming!" she called, and with a last look over her shoulder at him, walked away quickly.

Damn it to hell and back. Blake walked farther into the sections of the building where Charlie's rooms were. Her door was locked, the small waiting room, empty. He opened the curtains and looked outside. It was the usual Saturday-morning picture of a small-town street. But something was making him uneasy.

The coffee shop. That was what had been bothering him earlier, before he'd let his hormones take over his brain.

CHAPTER 5

Lindsay had her phone out and was dialing Brooke's number even before she greeted Lilly. She was burning up; her whole body seemed to be on fire. The look in Blake's eyes, his body pressed firmly against her, made it abundantly clear why he needed a minute. Air. Oh, goodness. She needed air.

Waving quickly at Lilly, she waited for Brooke to pick up. And why was it so hot? With her phone against her ear, she walked to the first window to open it.

"Let me…" Lilly said cheerily and quickly opened the window. "You looked flushed. What…?" Her eyes strayed over Lindsay's shoulder and widened. She grinned. "Oooh, now I understand those blushing cheeks." She giggled under her breath.

"Hi, Mr. Davidson…" Lilly sang, and walked over to him.

Lindsay turned away. Brooke wasn't picking up. She checked her watch. Brooke was probably busy with six-year-old Connor at this moment. Grimacing, she put her phone away and glanced over to where Lilly was chatting away with Blake. Why was he still here?

The bell above the door jingled. Plastering a smile on

43

her face, Lindsay turned around to greet her first customer of the day. A beaming Suzie Stevens rushed in.

"Lindsay!" she called, out of breath. "I have to tell you..." She inhaled on a laugh. "It was quite a night, my dear. Quite a night. I simply had to come and tell you about it."

Acutely aware of Blake's eyes on her, Lindsay tried her best to ignore him. "I'm so glad to hear that. So what can I do for you today?"

Suzie leaned forward. "I was hoping for another bottle of your bedroom oils. Tomorrow you're closed and...well, let's just say, I don't think there will be enough until Monday."

"Of course, you can have more, but you do know you only need a small amount of oil on your hands..."

"I know, dear, but it was going so well and..." Suzie grinned happily.

"Let me help, Mrs. Winters," Lilly interrupted, and smiled at Suzie before she looked at Lindsay. "Mr. Davidson wants to talk to you."

Lindsay felt like stamping her feet. Why hadn't Blake left already? There were people around her; he really didn't have to be here any longer.

"Is there a place where we can talk?" he asked as she neared him.

"I have a shop to run. I don't have time..."

"Damn it, Lindsay, will you please listen?" Taking her hand, he proceeded to walk in the direction of Charlie's rooms again.

"You had the whole morning to talk to me. Why...?"

He turned around and she lost her words. Pure, unadulterated hunger shone in his eyes, just for a millisecond, but she forgot where they were and why she'd been so worked up just now. But then it was gone and his lips formed the thin line she was used to.

"I shouldn't have touched you, I'm sorry. You make me feel things...and... Damn it, all I can think about is kissing you...but it's... I can't!" he called out in frustration.

Stunned, she stared at him. *Why does he keep talking about kissing me?* Around them, the air thickened. She had to say something before this got completely out of control. "I don't kiss men with beards," slipped out.

His eyes darkened. "I'll see you later today." And swearing softly, he turned and walked away.

Lindsay put her hand out to prop herself up against the wall, desperately trying to get enough oxygen into her lungs. Her legs felt like rubber; she wasn't sure she could walk just yet.

As long as she lived, she'd remember the look in his eyes. No man had ever looked at her in quite the same way, as if she were the most beautiful woman in the world and he wanted to devour her.

But he didn't want this—he'd just made that clear—and neither did she. The last time she'd given someone her heart, he'd trampled all over it, and the same person was still hell-bent on making her life miserable.

Her phone rang. It was Brooke. Inhaling slowly, she tried to find her equilibrium. Her phone kept ringing. Brooke. She wanted to ask her something. It was another second before she remembered why she'd called earlier.

"Hi, Brooke," she finally answered. "I have a favor to ask." She needed to put distance between herself and Blake as quickly as possible. And if she could sidestep Mark in the process, so much the better.

When Blake arrived at the dojo, Jason had just finished teaching a karate class. Blake nodded to the people leaving. Some faces were familiar; others he hadn't seen before.

"The classes have grown considerably since you've left." Jason greeted him with a handshake. "People from neighboring towns have heard about the dojo and have signed up. A high school came to investigate, and quite a number of their students enrolled afterwards."

"That's good news. I really appreciate you stepping in to help," Blake said.

"Of course. I'm enjoying my stay in Alisson. I may just decide to stay here after you sack me." Jason grinned.

"That's good to know. Our ex-employer needs help with another case, so I may need you again. Or have they contacted you, as well?"

Jason nodded. "About the bank robbers? Yeah, they did. I'm thinking about it. What about you?"

"Not until we find Taylor. Any news on that front?"

Jason shook his head. "After you phoned last night, I drove around town, but I didn't see the green car you described anywhere."

"Could be he left town. But he's nearby. I can feel it. I checked out the coffee shop across from Lindsay's shop this morning." He rubbed a hand over his neck. "I had this feeling someone was watching from inside. But by the time I got there, only the usual crowd were having their Saturday morning coffee. According to the waitress, there was someone earlier she doesn't know."

"So why did you get involved with this case? Hunting down ex-boyfriends isn't your usual gig, is it?" Jason asked with a twinkle in his eye.

"No. But I have to make sure she's safe."

Jason's eyes widened, and grinning, he slapped Blake on the shoulder. "You fell for a woman? Well, I never."

"No, I haven't fallen… What I mean is…" Whatever did he mean? "She's a friend."

Jason grinned. "A friend?" He sounded skeptical. "Okay. If you say so. Gorgeous friend, by the way."

Blake frowned. "I thought you told me she hasn't been for her self-defense classes since I've left."

"That doesn't mean I don't know who the most beautiful unattached female in town is."

Blake was staring at the door where a few women had entered, but his head whipped back to Jason when he registered what his friend had said. "Stay away from her," he growled before he could stop himself. He and Jason had worked together on numerous cases. He liked the tall, lanky guy, but he also knew there was a string of broken-hearted women in Jason's wake.

Jason laughed. "Thought so. You've got a thing for the lovely Lindsay?"

Blake shrugged. "Wouldn't matter if I did, would it? In our line of work…"

"But we've quit, remember? You don't have to take on the next case just because they ask you to."

"I have to."

Jason crossed his arms and leaned against the table. "Why?"

"Don't you have a class to teach?"

"Not right this minute, no."

"My partner died because I wasn't focused. So if I can help catch the next bad guy…" He shrugged.

Jason straightened. "That's not what happened, and you know it. Will made the decision to rush into a building and not wait for backup. That's not on you."

"I should've known what he was going to do. I should've stopped him."

"There was no way anyone could know what he was going to do."

"I was his partner…"

"Partner, yes. Keeper, no. Trying to get yourself killed, or trying to redeem yourself by continuously putting yourself in danger, is not going to bring your partner back. So you'll have to find another reason to stay away from the lovely Lindsay. Because I have to warn you, there are plenty others—me included—who wouldn't mind…"

"I said stay away from her."

"I'll stay away if you're making a move. Otherwise…" Jason taunted him.

"No. She deserves a whole lot better than a jaded ex-FBI agent like me or you."

He could hear Jason's laughter all the way back to his car. Damn it to hell. Before Miss Betty O'Hara had taken him in all those years ago, he'd learned the hard way, in the many, many homes he'd lived in for short periods of time, not to become too attached to anything or anyone. It could be taken away from him at any time. As was confirmed when first Miss Betty and then Will were killed.

He'd thought his strength and his fists could help him in any situation. But when Miss Betty fell ill and then died, or when Will stormed into that building and lost his life, there wasn't anything he could do. And the gut-wrenching pain he'd experienced when they'd died wasn't something he'd survive if there were a next time.

So he'd made sure to keep people at a distance, to not become involved with any woman for more than sex. That resolve had worked until he'd stepped into the bar in Alisson and had seen Lindsay Wilson for the first time.

She'd literally taken his breath away, and the clear lines he'd drawn to safeguard himself had been blurred. Cursing, he started his car. He had a window to replace and then he'd wait in the coffee shop until Lindsay was finished for the day. From there, he'd have a clear view of the shop, and she wouldn't know he was there.

Lilly locked the front door and walked back to where Lindsay was counting the money.

"Wow, we had a busy morning," Lilly said. "I love it. People love your products; we can hardly keep up. How did your chat with Stacy go? How soon can she create a website for all your lovely oils and creams?"

Lindsay smiled. Lilly's enthusiasm was one of her many endearing qualities. "We talked about what kind of look I'd want, the idea of a logo, and more or less what and how I'd want to do this. She'll send me some ideas and then we'll proceed from there."

Lilly rubbed her hands. "Ooh, so exciting!"

"Yes, it is. That's why I'm going to Seattle next week. I've made appointments with our suppliers. I need to get stock and just talk to them about my ideas."

Lilly frowned. "It sounds great, but should you leave now? When your ex is in town and looking for you?"

"A very good reason why I want to leave town now," Lindsay said. "Are you happy to run the shop on your own this week? I'm going to make a huge batch of creams this afternoon. It should be enough for the coming week. If you don't think you're up for it, we can always close the shop for a week."

"Never!" Lilly exclaimed. "It won't be the first time, remember. I've done this before, when you and Charlie and your brother went to Seattle."

"If you're sure, then great. I'm going with Eleanor and Brooke and we're leaving tomorrow morning. They'll probably stay a bit longer in Seattle, but I'll be back on Friday. You sure you'll be okay?"

Lilly took her bag from under the counter. "Of course. I'm off. I'll see you tonight at the bar?"

"Maybe not tonight. But next weekend when we're back."

"Have a great time!" With a wave, Lilly bounded out of the shop.

Lindsay sighed. Oh, to be so young and carefree again. Grimacing, she locked the front door. Twenty-six wasn't old; she just sometimes wished she'd never laid eyes on Mark Taylor. She'd like to be the carefree person she used to be before her world had changed forever.

She quickly looked around the shop. The windows were closed, the door locked; she could go to her studio. At this point, she was quite hungry, but she wanted to begin mixing the creams. Maybe she could slip out a little bit later.

The studio was small but ideal at the moment. She put her earphones on, picked out an album of the latest country artist she was enjoying, and sat down in front of the long bench where the magic happened.

Bliss. She didn't have to talk to anyone, the stupid butterflies were quiet, and she could do what she loved doing. She had still been a nursing sister back in South Africa when she'd been introduced to the age-old healing powers of essential oils, and after she'd bought a starter kit with a diffuser, she was hooked. Soon she was mixing oils and making skin products for everyone around her—until she'd met Mark. He quickly put an end to her plans of making it a business. It was a stupid idea, just what he'd expect from someone as stupid as her. He'd called her "stupid" so many times, she'd actually been at a point where she'd believed him.

But when she and Charlie had moved here from South Africa, she knew immediately that she wanted to work with essential oils. And here there were so many wonderful suppliers, she was in heaven. Finally, she was able to do something that gave her joy. Having her own shop, selling the creams she mixed by hand, seeing the pleasure on her client's faces were all her dreams come true. And it was going so well. Over the past few months, she'd had many visitors from out of town, people who'd heard about her products from locals.

Inhaling deeply, willing the bad thoughts away, she concentrated on the lovely voice of the artist singing in her ear about a woman who was crazy and beautiful, but he loved her anyway.

That was the kind of love her sister had found with Logan. They couldn't be more different, but Logan loved Charlie because of her uniqueness; he didn't ridicule or belittle her. And the way he looked at the woman he loved was the same way—

Her hands stilled.

Nah, she was being silly. It wasn't the way Blake looked at her at all. Besides, he may have had lustful thoughts at that moment, but it would be mostly because they'd been sharing the same space for a few hours. He was a man, she was a woman—these things happened but it didn't mean anything.

And he was very clear about the fact that nothing could happen between them.

But those few moments so very close to him... She groaned out loud. How was she ever going to forget his warm, throbbing body pressed against her?

CHAPTER 6

Blake sat in front of the window in the coffee shop. He had one eye on the shop and one on his computer when he saw Lilly leaving the premises. She had her bag over her shoulder. Did that mean she was leaving for the day? Damn it to hell.

He packed up his laptop and threw money on the table before he rushed outside. His coffee and sandwich had just arrived, but it was more important now to make sure Lindsay was okay.

Checking up and down the street, he strode across to Lindsay's shop. He could cheerily throttle her. Why the hell hadn't she told him she'd be alone this afternoon?

The door was locked. He peered through the window. No movement inside. Where did she go? He'd checked the back, but it was possible someone had slipped around the other corner.

He was jogging around the building before he'd finished the thought. Cold fingers clutched around his throat. If anything happened to Lindsay...

As he came around the corner of the building, he saw her through the window of a smaller building attached to the shop in front. She had earphones on her ears and was swaying to a sound only she could hear. Inhaling deeply, he closed his eyes for a moment. The damn woman was going to give him a heart attack.

He knocked on the window, but she didn't hear him. Hands on his hips, he stared at her. She was singing off key along with someone about "her crazy is beautiful to me." Cursing, he inhaled some fresh air. His self-appointed job to protect Lindsay was sure as hell going to kill him pretty soon.

At that moment, she opened her eyes and saw him. And shrieked. Still yelling, she pulled the earphones from her ears.

Great. But a yelling, angry Lindsay he could handle. It was the singing, swaying, crazy, and beautiful one who could bring him to his knees.

Lindsay opened the back door with unsteady fingers, her heart still pounding in her chest. She'd just had the fright of her life. The last person she'd expected to see through the window was Blake.

"You nearly gave me a heart attack," she scolded as he brushed past her.

"Good. Then we're even."

"I don't go sneaking around corners!"

"But you lied to me! Lilly has left."

"I didn't exactly lie. I said I won't be alone, and I'm not. There are people on either side of me."

"Oh, really?" He motioned with his hands. "The same people who've just come running because you've yelled?"

"I ..." Cross, she walked towards the counter where she was working. "I'm fine. Nobody else knows I'm here."

"Everybody who has been watching this building will know you're alone. Damn it, woman, do you have any idea how easy it would be for someone to get to you here if they wanted to? And that's exactly what Mark Taylor is trying to do, or haven't you noticed?"

Without any warning, the tears came out of nowhere. Sniffling, she turned her back on Blake. "Don't you think I know that? But I'm trying to get on with my life in spite of it. I refuse to allow him to frighten me again." In vain, she tried to mop up the tears, but it would seem she hadn't cried enough last night.

"Lindsay…" Blake began, behind her, before he cussed under his breath. "Please don't cry again." And two big, warm hands tentatively touched her shoulders.

Her whole being was urging her to turn around and bury her face in Blake's big, broad chest, but this was her mess and she was going to fix this.

Squaring her shoulders, she wiped her face. "I have to finish this. There isn't time during the week. I'll be fine."

The hands withdrew from her shoulders. Behind her, she heard movement and turned around. Blake put his laptop on a small desk near the window and took out his phone. "Have you eaten?"

She shook her head without looking at him and reheated the shea butter and coconut oil. If Blake hadn't disturbed her, she'd have been finished by now.

"What can I get you? I'm ordering from the coffee shop across the street."

"I'll go and fetch it…" she said.

"We either both go or I ask them to deliver it."

Shrugging, she turned her back on him and continued mixing the butter and oils. She had to finish this batch, otherwise there wouldn't be enough stock for the week.

"I'm ordering a coffee, and ham and cheese sandwich—what can I get you?"

"The same, thanks."

"Don't you prefer tea?"

She quickly glanced at him. "I do, but it doesn't really matter…"

"Of course, it matters what you want."

For a moment longer she stared at him, before she quickly turned back to what she was doing. Mark had never been in the least interested in what she'd preferred. He used to order for both of them without consulting her.

Minutes later, Blake had placed the order. "What can I do to help?" he asked.

Surprised, she looked at him. "It's not necessary…"

"I know. But I'm staying anyway so you may as well use me."

Use me. Her cheeks flamed and she leaned forward to hide them. The term had conjured up all sorts of playful ways in which she could "use" him. Times like these, she was indeed grateful thoughts couldn't be read or heard.

"Uhm…okay. If you could seal those lids…" She pointed towards a batch she'd made earlier. "I can finish up here."

They were working in silence when his phone rang. Happy to do something to distract himself, Blake quickly answered his phone.

For the last few minutes, he'd been watching Lindsay and she was driving him insane. While concentrating, her tongue would flicker out and lick her lips before it disappeared again. At this point, his body was ready to explode.

It was the coffee shop across the street. They were short-staffed at the moment. Could he please pick up the lunch order?

Blake put his phone away. "Let's lock up here and fetch lunch. The coffee shop doesn't have anyone to deliver it at the moment," he called out over the noise of the mixer Lindsay was using.

Not even looking up, she shook her head. "I can't stop now. The shop is just across the street. It'll only take a few minutes for you to fetch it. I'll be fine."

She continued mixing things even before she'd finished speaking.

Frowning, Blake stared at her back. He wasn't going to

get her out of here now, and they were both hungry. Damn it, he didn't want to leave her. But she was right—he should be back within minutes.

"Lock behind me!" he called as he left.

As he crossed the street, an uneasiness settled in his gut, a telltale sign something was wrong. After scanning the street a few times, he finally walked into the shop.

The waiter behind the counter recognized him and lifted a package. "Here's your lunch. Sorry about that."

As Blake took out his wallet, he glanced out the window. Everything looked all right, but the little voice he usually relied on, telling him to hurry, was getting louder by the minute.

Lindsay glanced at the door. She had to lock it, but she was so close to finishing mixing this batch of shea butter and oils. By this time she knew exactly what consistency she wanted and if she stopped the mixer too soon, the content wouldn't have the lovely fluffy and smooth texture her creams were known for.

Minutes later, she smiled. Now this was more like it. She switched off the mixer and dipped a clean finger in to touch. As she rubbed it into her hands, she caught a movement from the corner of her eye and quickly looked up. Frowning, she walked over to the window.

Nothing strange. She was so sure she'd seen something.

Rubbing her arms, she walked back to the counter where she'd been working. She was becoming paranoid.

Blake glanced up and down the street before he began to cross it. As he looked up, a car pulled quickly out of a parking space just a few meters from Lindsay's shop and sped down the street—much too fast. His heart stopped before it nearly jumped out of his throat.

Repeating the plate number over and over, he clutched

the bag and sped across the street. *Lindsay*. If something had happened to her during the time he'd been away…

As he rounded the corner of the building, he began shouting her name. "Lindsay! Lindsay!" He pushed at the door and it swung open.

She turned around, her eyes wide with trepidation.

"Why the hell didn't you lock the door?" he bellowed as he marched towards her.

"Don't yell at me!" she cried out, rubbing her arms. Lifting her chin, she picked up one of the many glass jars she used for the creams. "I wanted to finish the batch I was working on." But her voice wobbled slightly and her hands weren't quite steady.

Inhaling deeply, he tried to calm the thunderous beating of his heart. "Did you see something outside?" he asked, in a much gentler tone.

She opened and closed her mouth. "I was just being paranoid, I think," she finally said.

An imaginary yet icy hand closed around his trachea. "Damn it to hell, Lindsay…" he growled, exasperated, and rubbed his face.

"Have you brought lunch?" she asked as she continued to spoon heaps of cream into jars. "I'm hungry."

"What did you see, or think you saw?"

She motioned towards the one window. "Seriously, Blake, it was probably only my imagination."

"Lindsay…"

"Okay, I thought I saw a movement outside"—she motioned with her hand—"but as I've said…"

Before she'd finished speaking, he'd put the bag with lunch down and headed outside. Crouching down close to the window she'd pointed to, he inspected the area outside.

And there it was—the evidence they'd been looking for. Below the window, in the flower bed, were the indentations of fresh shoe prints. There weren't any other prints around. Someone had stood right here, watching

Lindsay. Cold fury leaped up, but he pushed it down, and straightening, he took out his phone and dialed Jason's number.

"Did you find anything?" Lindsay spoke while he was waiting for Jason to answer. She was standing in the door, chewing her lip, looking heartbreakingly beautiful.

He shook his head, not even sure what she'd asked. As she headed back into the shop, Jason finally answered his call. *Focus on the task at hand.* And the task at hand was protecting Lindsay. Not lusting after her.

By the time they arrived back home, Lindsay looked pale. She kept rubbing her temple; she was probably experiencing the beginnings of a headache.

Jason had agreed to find out to whom the number plates were registered, so at least now Blake could concentrate on keeping Lindsay safe. Not that she was making it easy.

He'd wanted to get her back to her house, but she'd insisted on finishing filling the jars with the last batch of creams she'd made, and they'd worked in silence until she was happy. Why the hell it couldn't be done later, he had no idea, but he'd given up long ago trying to understand the workings of the female mind.

He for one was glad they'd left the small, intimate studio. Working so close to her, surrounded by the flowery scent that always seemed to accompany her, made it extremely difficult to concentrate on anything else.

This time, he was quick enough to open the car door for her.

"Do you want to go out tonight?" he asked when they reached the front door.

She shook her head while unlocking the door.

"I bought steaks earlier and can do those over the grill if you like?" he asked when they'd entered the house.

She nodded. "Okay. Please let me pay half?"

"Don't be ridiculous. What would you like with it?"

"I'll do something with potatoes. I just want to have a shower…"

The groan slipped out before he could stop it. Startled blue eyes looked up at him before she turned around and jogged up the stairs.

Damn. Exhaling slowly, he opened the front door again and walked around the house. Picturing a naked Lindsay in the shower came way too easily to mind.

It was already dark. For a few minutes, he stood at the back of the house, focusing on his breathing, hoping to get the rhythm of his heart back to normal.

He bent down and checked the pane of the window he'd replaced earlier that day. The light at the back of the house was bright enough. At the time, he'd also looked around on the ground outside the window but he hadn't found anything out of the ordinary. There were no footprints, no indication anyone had stood there before the stone had been thrown through the window.

He wanted to do something—break, kick, hit. That was what he was good at. Waiting, playing cat and mouse, was part of the job, something he'd had to get used to, but he hated the frustration. Especially now, because Lindsay was involved.

It was fast becoming clear to him Taylor was a shrewd and probably unhinged adversary. And as he knew from experience, those were the deadliest.

Taylor seemed to disappear into thin air after every incident. They'd caught the guy who'd hit Charlie months earlier and he was awaiting trial, but not talking, so there was nothing the police could find to link the man to Mark Taylor, and as far as he knew, the police had dropped the matter.

But Blake had asked his informant to keep checking flights from South Africa. And when he'd received the message Taylor had boarded a plane heading first to Houston, then to Seattle, he knew his gut feeling had been right.

But the man seemed to be two steps ahead of them all the time. The police couldn't find the green car he'd seen yesterday, but today a faded blue one had been parked in front of Lindsay's shop. Although he hadn't seen Taylor, he just knew he was the one who'd been trying to get to Lindsay. And by tomorrow he'd probably have a different car again.

So far nobody had been able to get a trace of him. The shoe marks he'd found at the back of Lindsay's shop had been the first real, tangible evidence. Since yesterday, the police had scoured the town and the neighboring areas, but they hadn't found the green car or the man yet.

Hopefully now that Jason had agreed to help him, they could get this guy. That was what his phone call earlier to Jason had been about. His friend had promised to get forensics to analyze the footprints, as well.

Taylor's plan to scare and keep Lindsay on edge was working, and he hated that.

He turned his head and listened. Evenings in Alisson were quiet, he'd discovered in the short time he'd spent here previously. He could hear the odd vehicle now and then. Behind the curtains of the houses on either side of this one, there was movement, but otherwise it was quiet.

He stared up at the sky. In another world, another life, maybe he and Lindsay could've... Thinking like that was pointless, as he very well knew. Cursing, he walked back into the house.

CHAPTER 7

As Lindsay came down the stairs, heavenly smells wafted towards her from the direction of the kitchen. She'd taken longer than usual, but she'd also quickly packed a suitcase and stored it in the bathroom. Hopefully she'd manage to sneak out tomorrow morning before Blake woke up.

He was standing with his back to her in front of the grill, a kitchen cloth over his shoulder. In a white short-sleeve T-shirt and low-slung jeans, which fitted perfectly around a sexy ass, he looked right at home behind the stove.

His hair was still wet; he'd also taken a shower. Images of his wet, naked body flashed in front of her eyes. Her knees buckled and she had to hold on to the kitchen counter to make sure she didn't fall flat on her face. Ever since the extreme close-up she'd had with Blake, she hadn't been able to get those few seconds out of her head.

"Ready for a glass of wine?" he asked as he turned around.

She nodded, unable to utter one word. For one, her mouth was way too dry and her brain seemed to have stopped working altogether. He handed her a glass of wine and their fingers touched.

Quickly she turned away. "Salad. I'll make…" But in her haste, she knocked over a small jug and the contents spilled out all over the counter. "I'm sorry…" She reached to grab a dishcloth to clean up the mess.

But hers hadn't been the only hand reaching for it, and Blake's warm fingers grazed her skin. They both inhaled sharply and chocolate brown eyes met hers.

"I…I'll clean it up," she got out, not quite sure what she was talking about. His beard looked soft. She could test and make sure. Maybe if she lifted herself on her toes…

"Don't look at me like that," he said softly, and took the cloth from her. "I'll clean up. I'll make more sauce for the steak. You go make the salad."

With her heart hammering away like crazy, Lindsay got the ingredients for a salad from the fridge. The light in Blake's eyes… Her poor heart wasn't sure whether to skip, tumble, or just stagger to a halt.

By the time they sat down to eat, Blake's jaw was hurting from gnashing his teeth. If he didn't break a few tonight, it would be a miracle. Damn, he hadn't behaved like a hormone-filled teenager in a long time, but around Lindsay, his body seemed hell-bent on taking over the workings of his mind.

He had to finish his dinner and get away from her, for both their sakes. Everything in him was urging him to pick her up and take her up the stairs and show her what she was doing to him. He'd never been good with words, but he could express what was inside him with his hands and mouth and body and…

Grinding his teeth again, he tried to focus on his food. But he couldn't touch her. Ever. Once would never be enough with her. Besides, apart from the fact that this was a tension-filled situation and the desire he saw in Lindsay's eyes was probably only because of everything that had happened since she'd heard from her ex, he'd long ago decided anything long-term wasn't for him.

Love and family could never be part of his future. He wouldn't know how to be a husband or a dad.

Husband? Dad? Where the hell had that thought come from?

All he knew about love and family was the short time he'd lived with Miss Betty. Even though he'd been an angry and bitter teenager, trying to make everyone's life around him as miserable as his own had been, she'd shown him kindness and loved him and had gradually managed to tear down the walls he'd erected around his heart.

And then she'd died. He'd been eighteen and finally able to escape the system. That was when he'd joined the army and eventually ended up with the FBI, where his partner Will Miller became his family, his brother, his friend. Until Will had died, too.

Pushing the memories away, he gulped down his dinner in record time. He'd probably end up having indigestion, but it was a whole lot better than doing something he knew he'd regret later.

Wiping his mouth with a napkin, he quickly got up. "Excuse me. Jason was going to find out about the shoe print under your window..." He swallowed the rest of his words, but it was too late. Oh, damn, he hadn't wanted her to know about it.

Startled blue eyes looked up at him. She'd hardly eaten anything yet. "What shoe print?"

"On the ground under the window outside your studio."

Slowly she got up, as well. "Why didn't you tell me? And why ask Jason? Why not tell the police?"

"I...know Jason well. We've worked together before and I know he'll go the extra mile. I trust him. I didn't tell you because I was going to wait until I hear b—" Before he could finish, his phone rang. "It's him."

"Please put it on speaker," she said firmly, and moved closer.

He pressed the speaker before he answered. "Jason. Lindsay is also listening." Jason would get the message not to reveal anything that might upset her.

Blake was holding the phone and had turned his hand so that Lindsay could also hear what Jason was saying. She'd seen the tall, lanky man around town, but she'd never actually met him. What kind of work had Blake and Jason done before? Would their previous job be the reason Blake had disappeared over the past few months?

"Okay, so it was a size twelve shoe, but we have to wait to hear from forensics if they can get anything else from the print," Blake was saying. "What about the license plates?"

"Fake, of course," Jason said.

Blake sighed. "Of course, they would be. Damn it." Blake lifted a hand, rubbed the back of his neck. "Anything else?"

But Jason didn't have any other news. The two men began to talk about the dojo. She should move away; there wasn't any need for her to stay this close to Blake. But her feet felt heavy, ignoring all the messages from her brain as her eyes focused on Blake's long fingers, moved up his forearm, and then even farther up to feast on his broad shoulders. And when she turned her head slightly, the outline of a perfectly muscled six-pack under the white T-shirt was right in front of her eyes. Would it feel as hard as it looked?

"I'll see you tomorrow," Blake was saying, and looked up. His eyes were on her. He ended the call.

"Go to bed, please?" His voice was low, sending shivers down her spine.

Why was she standing so close to him? Mortified, she turned away. "I'll clean up."

For a few minutes it was quiet.

"See you in the morning." His smooth whiskey voice nearly made her turn around again. The next minute she heard footsteps leaving. Fast.

She sagged against the kitchen counter, feeling light-headed. That had been a very close call. If he'd stayed a second longer, she'd have flung herself into his arms. Her legs refused to keep her upright any longer and she pulled the chair out. She'd hardly touched her dinner. But food wasn't going to help. The ache in her belly had nothing whatsoever to do with food.

Thank goodness she was leaving tomorrow. There was no way she could stay in the same house as Blake for another day and not do something very stupid.

Rubbing her temple, she exhaled slowly. Think. Be logical. Her reaction to Blake was quite understandable. He was ridiculously attractive and sexy, and she hadn't been with anyone for a long time. Add the very stressful situation they were in at the moment and her intense emotions and wayward hormones could be explained.

Surely once Mark had been caught, she'd be able to forget about Blake within a day or so. Okay, she hadn't forgotten about him while he'd been away for those three months, but there were all sorts of explanations for that. With Charlie getting married…

Which reminded her, she'd been meaning to let Charlie know about her plans to visit them, but this morning she'd been so flustered and this afternoon she'd been focused on finishing filling the jars.

With still unsteady fingers, she picked up her phone. Her sister answered after one ring.

"What happened?" Charlie asked, her voice immediately laced with concern.

"I'm fine. But we think Mark was around this afternoon while I was working in the studio."

"What do you mean you 'think'?"

Quickly, Lindsay explained what had happened earlier

and the footprints Blake had found in the flower bed.

"Oh, Linds," Charlie cried out. "Why can't the police find and stop the bloody man?"

"Good question. And that's why I've decided to go with Eleanor and Brooke tomorrow when they visit you guys. I'm quite happy to stay elsewhere if you don't have enough room…"

"Don't be silly. There's more than enough room for everyone in Logan's apartment, and I'll feel a whole lot better if I have eyes on you. But, Linds, is that the best thing to do right now? What does Blake say about your coming to Seattle?"

"Blake can't forever be stuck here with me; he needs to get on with his life and so do I. So how's Baby?"

Charlie laughed. "Talking about Baby isn't always going to work. But Baby is fine, growing by the day."

Blake's body was still not back to normal when he headed down the stairs again. He wanted to check the street again while Lindsay was in the kitchen. How he'd managed to walk away from her minutes earlier, he still didn't quite know.

No woman had ever had this effect on him. He liked sex, loved kissing women, but this weird connection, for lack of a better description, he felt with Lindsay was way beyond anything he'd experienced before. And he knew if he kissed her it wasn't going to end there.

As he neared the lower steps, he heard Lindsay's voice.

"Blake can't forever be stuck here with me; he needs to get on with his life and so do I," Lindsay was saying. "So how's Baby?"

Frowning, he opened the front door and walked outside. The "how's Baby" meant Lindsay was talking to Charlie. But why would she mention he needed to get on with his life? An uneasiness settled in his gut. She was up to something. The question was, what?

Outside, he walked out into the street and looked up and down. He'd made a mental note of the types of cars Lindsay's neighbors drove, and at the moment there weren't any strange cars in sight.

As he walked back towards the house, Lindsay's words replayed over and over again. Getting on with his life...

Once Mark Taylor was caught, there wouldn't be any reason to be in Lindsay's life. A hole the size of Texas opened up inside him. Rubbing his chest, he swore. He wasn't getting involved with Lindsay or any other woman. Ever.

Maybe if he kept reminding him of his resolve, these strange feelings would eventually go away. They had to.

CHAPTER 8

The next morning, when Lindsay got into the back of Brooke's car, it was a quarter past six and still dark. The flight to Bozeman was scheduled to leave at quarter to eight. Eleanor was sitting in front next to Brooke, and Brooke's six-year-old son was also in the back.

"Thanks for picking me up," Lindsay said. "I really could've come to your house."

In fact, she'd tried very hard to convince Brooke to let her do that, but both Eleanor and Brooke insisted they'd pick her up. Both women were artists and self-confessed free spirits, which meant time didn't really have any meaning for them—as she and Charlie had discovered over the last two years. Lindsay, on the other hand, was worried they'd all be late.

But her main concern had been that Blake would wake up. She'd showered last night and hadn't even made herself a cup of coffee in fear he'd hear the noise. By some miracle he hadn't woken up, and yes, Eleanor and Brooke were about fifteen agonizing minutes late, but there was still plenty of time to get to the airport in Bozeman.

"No trouble." Brooke smiled.

"Hi, Lindsay." Brooke's six-year old Connor smiled

sleepily. "Mommy said you'll be sitting with me."

Reaching out to the little boy, Lindsay touched his hand. "Of course I will." Connor had a blanket, and within minutes he was sleeping, his head dropping towards her shoulder. An unexpected lump in her throat forced her to swallow a few times.

She loved children, always had. It was part of why she'd become a nurse. But after her experience with Mark... How could she ever trust a man again? Trust her own feelings? But if she never opened up her heart to someone else, she'd never be able to have children. Was that really the life she wanted?

"I was wondering what Blake has to say about your visit to Seattle?" Eleanor asked as they drove away. She was sitting in the front of the car, next to Brooke, and had turned around. "Wasn't he upset?"

"Uhm...well, he doesn't know," Lindsay confessed.

Eleanor's eyes widened. "You haven't told him?"

Lindsay shook her head. "We have no idea when the police will catch Mark and, well...Blake has his own life to get back to."

"But you've left him a note?" Brooke asked.

"Well...uhm...no..."

Eleanor looked at her sternly. "That's not very nice, is it? He moved into your house to make sure nothing will happen to you. When he wakes up and you're not there, he'll be so worried."

Lindsay swallowed a sigh and took out her phone. Eleanor was right, she knew it; she'd been agonizing over it since the day before. "Okay, I'll text him."

"Shame. He's gone out of his way to look after you. He'll probably be frantic with worry when he discovers you're not there." Eleanor was smiling, but the censure in her tone couldn't be missed.

Lindsay's finger hovered over her phone. She had thought of leaving a note, but she didn't know what to say and she still wasn't sure. After another few seconds, she finally typed a short message before she put her phone away.

Blake opened his eyes. Something was wrong. He jumped out of bed and raced to Lindsay's room. The door was open, her bed neatly made up, but she wasn't there.

Damn it to hell. He'd struggled to sleep the night before and had only fallen asleep around four. He should've heard her when she'd moved around. She'd probably made a point of moving around silently, but he was trained to pick up noises; he should've heard her.

With his heart hammering in his ears, he charged out of her room and down the stairs. "Lindsay! Lindsay!" he called, switching on lights as he went.

But she wasn't in the house. He'd actually known it the minute he'd opened his eyes. Where had she gone? Or had someone taken her? No, her bed was made up; it couldn't be that.

Frantically, he looked around in the kitchen. She hadn't even left a damn note. Maybe a text?

He sprinted out of the kitchen, up the stairs, and as he entered his room, his phone lit up and bleeped. A message. Hands shaking, he picked up his phone. From Lindsay. Quickly, he opened it.

On my way to Seattle with Brooke and Eleanor. Thanks.

He let out a frustrated roar, and grabbing his keys, he raced out of his room and down the stairs, his heart hammering away. If anything were to happen to Lindsay...

It was quiet in the car. Lindsay felt awful. She'd closed her eyes and was resting her head against the seat. It was clear both Eleanor and Brooke were upset because she hadn't told Blake she was going to visit her sister. And sitting here, it seemed so obvious she should've told him. But the only thought she'd had yesterday was to get away from him as quickly and as far as possible, because he was making her feel things she'd never felt before.

There, she'd acknowledged it. But she didn't have to say it out loud. Because it wasn't real. Because it was temporary. She knew it, he knew it. That was why, in spite of his obvious desire for her, he'd walked away from her time and time again whereas she would've happily thrown herself into his arms, if he'd been willing.

Which he hadn't been.

"Anything wrong, Brooke?" Eleanor broke the silence.

Lindsay opened her eyes.

"I'm not sure," Brooke said, checking the rear window constantly. "But I've noticed lights behind us. Not strange, I know, but whoever is driving the car behind us has kept his distance so far. It's just…over the last few minutes, the car has increased speed and is now nearly on top of us. I'm not sure whether it wants to overtake us or…"

Lindsay turned around. A pair of very bright lights were approaching fast. It was possibly only someone driving faster than they were but what if… Her breath hitched in her throat and Blake's words echoed in her mind: *You'll be putting other people in danger, as well.*

Oh, damn, she'd been so intent on getting away from Blake and the crazy feelings he was stirring inside her, she never considered the possibility Mark might have been watching her. What if he was driving the car behind them?

"I'm phoning Blake and then the police," Eleanor said, her phone already against her ear.

Blake's anger lasted until he'd left Alisson's lights behind him. And then cold fear threatened to cut off his oxygen.

If Taylor had been keeping an eye on Lindsay's movements—and at this point it was obvious that was what he was doing—he would know she'd left Alisson in a car. And there were two other women and probably

Brooke's son also in the car.

Minutes ago, when he'd driven away from Lindsay's home, he'd phoned Jason and asked him to contact the police in Livingston, the next town on their way to Bozeman. He had no idea at what time the women had left Alisson, but he'd checked the details on his phone and established there was a flight that morning to Seattle at a quarter to eight, which meant they'd probably left about fifteen minutes before he woke up.

With his eyes on the road in front of him, his heart in his throat, he tried to concentrate on his driving. If anything were to happen to Lindsay...

He went around a bend in the road, and for the first time he saw two sets of car lights in the distance in front of him. Just then his phone rang. It was Eleanor.

"Blake...where are you?"

"Behind you."

"Please hurry. Brooke is driving, but the car behind us..." And then she yelped. The line went dead.

Blake gritted his teeth and stepped on the gas.

Lindsay and Connor were thrown forward. Shocked, she glanced over her shoulder as she held on tightly to Connor's hand. They'd seen the lights approaching faster and faster but she hadn't expected the car would intentionally ram into Brooke's.

There could be no doubt anymore that the person driving the car behind them was either Mark, or someone he'd paid to get to her. And she'd put everyone in the car in danger because she hadn't thought it through.

Muttering, Brooke clutched her hands around the steering wheel and stepped on the gas. Brooke's car surged forward, leaving the other car behind, but within seconds it had also increased speed and was again gaining up on them.

"Lights in front!" Eleanor called out. "Put on your

hazard lights!"

Brooke pushed a button and the lights from the car began to flash.

While still holding Connor tightly against her, Lindsay turned around again. "There is another car coming up behind this one," she said and watched as another set of lights approached.

"Hopefully, that's Blake," Eleanor said, looking over her shoulder. "He told me he was right behind us."

"I'm going to stop," Brooke said, and the car began to slow down.

She pulled off the road and the next moment, the car behind them zipped past. In that millisecond, Lindsay could clearly see the driver's face. It was Mark.

The other car they'd noticed pulled in behind them, and the door opened. With her heart hammering, Lindsay stared at the tall figure getting out of the car. Blake.

"Look, the coming car has also stopped," Eleanor said and pointed to the opposite side of the road. "It's a police car. Blake probably called them."

"Mommy?" A sleepy Connor rubbed his eyes. "Are we at the airport?"

Brooke turned to Connor and patted his arm. No, we're not at the airport yet."

The next moment, the door on Lindsay's side flew open and Blake dragged her from the vehicle. His breath was coming out in gasps, and for long seconds, his eyes raked over her. "Are you okay?"

She couldn't speak, just nodded.

With a groan, he pulled her into his arms. "What the hell, Lindsay, you'll be the death of me yet," he murmured while he ran his hands over her arms, down her body before he looked at her again. "Are you sure you're okay? You weren't hurt?"

"I'm so sorry..." she began, but he bent his head and warm, urgent lips captured hers. She gasped; his tongue ploughed into her mouth as he deepened the kiss. His beard brushed against her skin, adding another sensation she hadn't expected.

Someone cleared his throat loudly near them and Blake dropped his arms. Still breathing heavily, he raked a hand through his hair before he turned away. For the first time, she saw the policeman standing next to them.

Eleanor was getting out of the car.

Lindsay rushed towards her. "I'm so sorry. This is all my fault. I should never..." A sob escaped.

The older woman pulled her into a hug. "This is not on you. The driver in that car is the one with the problem. Did you see who it was?"

Lindsay pulled out of her friend's hug and nodded. "It was Mark. I can't believe he'd go to such lengths..."

Blake approached them slowly. Behind him, the policeman was on his phone.

He greeted everyone before he bent and looked into the car. "Brooke...are you okay?"

"That was frightening, but we're okay," she replied. "I seriously hope someone catches that guy soon. He's obviously unstable."

Blake crouched down beside the car. "Hey, Connor? You doing okay?" His voice was soft.

"Where is the airport?" Connor asked.

Brooke smiled and ruffled his head. "We're not there yet, sweetie. Mom? You okay?" she asked as she leaned forward to look at Eleanor, who was still standing outside. Blake got up.

"Blake?" Eleanor asked. "What do you think? Will he try something again?"

He shook his head. "I don't know. Let me check the rear of your car." Brooke also got out, and they all moved to the back of the car to see what damage had been done. Blake introduced them all to Jim, the policeman.

"Tell you what. I'll get this fixed—" Blake began.

"I'm sure we could drive to the airport—" Brooke began.

But he shook his head. "Let me do this, please? I'll drive you to Bozeman, and when you need to return, I'll come and pick you up. You just tell me when."

"Thank you," Eleanor said. "I'll text you the details."

They all helped to move the luggage to Blake's car, and within minutes they were on the road again, the lights of Jim's cruiser behind them. He was going to follow them to the airport.

Rattled, confused, and upset, Lindsay closed her eyes for a minute before she took a deep breath. She owed everyone an apology. "Eleanor and Brooke—I am so sorry. Blake told me not to put other people in danger but I…I'm sorry." Peering up at the rearview mirror, she looked at the silent man behind the wheel. "I'm sorry. I should've told you I was going to Seattle."

His eyes met hers. "Yeah. You should've. Get some rest."

By the time he stopped in front of Bozeman Yellowstone International airport, Blake's heart rate was still not back to normal. He hoped never to experience the sheer terror of earlier ever again.

That moment he saw the one car ramming into the one in front…his heart had simply stopped beating for a few seconds. That was when he'd begun to suspect Taylor, or someone he'd paid, was behind the job. Lindsay had just confirmed that it had been Taylor himself. But the damn coward had quickly escaped when he'd noticed the two other cars.

Things could so easily have been much worse. If he hadn't woken up in time early that morning, if Lindsay hadn't sent him a text, finally telling him where she was going, if he hadn't phoned the police in Livingston…

They all got out. "Let me help with the luggage," he said. "What about a cart?"

"Good idea," Eleanor said. "We have small bags, but

Brooke has more than one bag to manage."

He grabbed the closest cart and quickly put all the bags on it. As long as he stayed busy, he was okay. Then he didn't have to think about what had nearly happened, about Lindsay leaving…

"Blake?" Jim, the policeman, called from his car. "I'm on my way. I'll talk to you later."

He nodded. Jim had to get back to his work and he had to get back to Alisson. He'd bet the coward was on his way back there. He'd lie in wait. He would know Lindsay would have to return sometime.

"See you soon!" Eleanor said as she hugged him.

"Let me know when I can pick you up," he said as Brooke also gave him a quick hug.

"That'll be wonderful, thanks." Brooke smiled before she took Connor's hand.

"I'll take the cart," Lindsay said and put her bag on top of the other luggage.

"Lindsay…"

She turned to him, her hands on the metal handle.

"Look after yourself," he murmured, and kissed her. There was no way he could let her go without having another taste of her.

Her mouth was soft and warm, and opened up for him. For a second their tongues touched before he lifted his head. "I…" But he couldn't ever tell her how much he wanted her at this moment. "I have to go."

"Thank you. I'm so sorry…"

He brushed a wayward curl behind her ears. "I'll see you soon."

CHAPTER 9

A very worried Charlie was waiting for them at Seattle-Tacoma Airport. Logan was standing a little bit behind, talking on his phone. The moment he saw them, though, he finished his call and welcomed them with open arms. His mother and sister both rushed into his embrace.

Charlie held out her arms, and with a soft cry, Lindsay walked into her sister's hug.

"Blake has just spoken to Logan," Charlie said, rubbing her back. "I can't believe what that damn Mark has tried to do! You okay?"

Sniffling, Lindsay nodded, and lifted her head to greet Logan. "I feel absolutely terrible for putting your mom and sister in danger. I just didn't think he—"

"Let's not think about all the what-ifs," Logan said. "You're here and you're all safe. Let's get you home."

Lindsay ended up in the back of Logan's car between Brooke, Connor, and Charlie.

"How are you feeling?" she asked Charlie.

Grinning, Charlie patted her still-flat tummy. "I'm twenty weeks and happy to say I'm not nauseous any longer and have my appetite back. At the moment, Baby is about the size of an apple and..." Her smile widened.

81

"I've felt some wiggling and movement."

Lindsay smiled. "Really?"

"And we'll be able to find out the gender by next week—I can't wait to know."

"It's a little girl with her mama's blue eyes." Logan grinned.

"Or a little boy with his daddy's blue eyes," Charlie teased, and touched her husband's back from behind.

Eleanor had more questions about the pregnancy and an excited Charlie was happy to comply. Leaning back against the car seat, Lindsay touched her mouth. She couldn't be happier for Charlie but somewhere deep inside her a sadness had settled.

Babies. She'd thought she'd come to grips with the idea of not ever getting married and having them, but ever since she'd met Blake, she kept thinking about happy-ever-after and making babies.

Her lips were still tingling from Blake's kiss. Wow. Two kisses within the span of about an hour. Well, she had wondered what it would be like to kiss Blake. Now she knew—it wasn't like any other kiss she'd had before.

Swallowing a groan, she closed her eyes. Within seconds, her thoughts had jumped from having babies to Blake kissing her.

"Lindsay," Connor's voice penetrated her thoughts, "you look sad."

She opened her eyes and touched the little boy's nose. "I'm fine."

He stared at her with big eyes. "Didn't Blake kiss it better?"

"What?" Charlie leaned forward. "What did Blake kiss better?" she asked Connor.

Connor pointed. "Lindsay."

Charlie looked at her with raised eyebrows. "Really?"

Connor nodded solemnly and held up two fingers. "Two times."

"He was just worried," Lindsay said quickly. "We were

all a bit rattled."

"I didn't get a kiss," Eleanor said.

"Neither did I," nodded Brooke. "And I was the one driving."

"Lindsay?" Charlie asked. "So why is Blake kissing you?"

"It was... We both had a fright; it's really no big deal," Lindsay said and crossed her arms.

Logan chuckled. "Don't tell me we're having another wedding before Christmas?"

"Of course not!" Lindsay called out, upset. "For some or other reason, he feels he needs to protect me."

"Wonder why?" Charlie teased.

"Something to do with his previous job, whatever that was," Lindsay mumbled.

"I think Logan knows what he used to do for a living..." Charlie said.

"...But I'm not talking." Logan shrugged. "He'll tell you in his own time. Okay, gals, where shall we go for lunch. Mom?"

Lindsay stared straight ahead and the voices around her faded. What kind of job had Blake done? Whatever it had been, he seemed to be able to find out things about other people and contact police at any given time and in any town or city.

And he'd kissed her. Oh, my goodness, she was thinking of the kiss again. Aargh!

For the rest of the day, Blake kept busy. When he'd left Bozeman that morning, he'd organized the local mechanic to tow Brooke's car to his workshop. Hopefully, her car would be ready by the time the women returned for the weekend.

He spent the rest of the day at the dojo so that Jason could have some free time. He'd thrown himself into the classes to try and keep himself from worrying about

Lindsay. The Livingston police had phoned earlier. They'd been on the lookout for Taylor's car, but hadn't seen the one similar to the one Blake had described.

By eight o'clock in the evening, he parked next to Lindsay's house. He wanted to pick up his stuff and make sure the house was properly locked before he went back to his own place.

Once inside, he checked all the windows and doors and headed up the stairs to get his bag and leave, but somehow, he ended up in Lindsay's room. Her scent still lingered in the room, instantly heating his blood.

The space was decorated in soft pink-and-grey colors, clean lines, no frills except for the lace pillows on the bed, and lace curtains in front of the windows. Feminine, alluring, beautiful—like Lindsay.

Taking out his phone, he sat down on her bed. For long minutes he stared at the small screen. He shouldn't have kissed her that morning, but he'd been out of his mind with worry. To see her getting out of the car, seemingly unscathed, had simply wiped his usual logical mind to the side, and he'd finally given in to the urge to touch her.

It hadn't been a conscious decision; it had just happened. And since then, he couldn't think of anything else.

Cussing, he began typing a message. He wanted to make sure she was okay after the morning's ordeal; that was the only reason he was texting her now.

With his phone in his hand, he lay back on the bed. *Mmm, nice mattress.*

By half past nine in the evening, Lindsay closed the bedroom door behind her. Logan had taken them to lunch earlier and they'd just had a light supper. Logan, his mother, and sister were still chatting, but when Charlie had excused herself, Lindsay had also jumped up.

Since the morning, she hadn't had a minute alone and she needed to think. She walked to the big windows overlooking the city. Damn Mark Taylor! All through the day, she'd found herself glancing over her shoulder. She hated having to live like this.

And she still felt terrible about scaring Eleanor and Brooke. Fortunately, Connor had been asleep and had no recollection of the incident.

So where was Mark at this very moment? Had he gone back to Alisson? Or had he somehow discovered they were in Seattle and followed her here? Rubbing her temple, she sat down on the bed and took out her phone. Maybe Blake would know.

Before she even opened her phone, she saw his message, sent at around eight. Quickly, she opened it.

Are you okay?

Her heart sighed and she typed a reply.

I'm fine. Have you heard anything from the police?

For minutes she sat staring at the phone before she jumped up. Blake was probably out, or busy.

She unpacked but took her phone with into the bathroom. She was going to take a long, hot bath. Hopefully, it would help her to relax.

Disoriented, Blake woke up. He was still in Lindsay's room—on Lindsay's bed. Grabbing his phone, he sat up. She'd sent a message, wanted to know what the police said.

And then, he simply had to hear her voice. He phoned. She picked up after one ring.

"Blake?"

Water? Was that what he heard. So it meant she... He inhaled sharply. "Are you in the bath?"

"Uhm…yes."

Shaking his head, he swore softly. "Do you have any idea what the image of you in a bath does to me?"

"Blake…" Her soft voice in his ear sent his blood

boiling. She inhaled shakily. "Where are you?"

"On your bed."

"My bed?"

"Yeah. Your bed. I came to get my bag but then I walked into your room, sat down on your bed and...I must've fallen asleep."

"It's a nice bed."

"It's a very nice bed."

For a few moments it was silent. But he could hear her moving in the bath. Damn.

"Jim phoned," he said, to distract himself from the noises of her splashing.

"Jim?"

"Policeman from this morning?"

"Oh, yes. Anything?"

"I'm afraid not."

"Do you know where Mark is?"

"No."

Again, it was quiet for a few minutes.

"You kissed me," she said.

"I did."

"Twice."

"Indeed."

"Why?"

"I...I was worried about you."

"Do you kiss everyone you're worried about?"

Thinking of the many weird characters he'd worried about at some time or another over the span of his life, he had to grin. "No."

"That's not an answer!" she called out.

"That's my answer." He waited a beat. "For now."

He rubbed his face. What the hell was he doing? Flirting with Lindsay? He knew better than most that in these kind of tense situations, feelings were seldom real.

Whatever this was, it was temporary. And even if it was something deeper, he could never again allow anyone to depend on him. There were two dead bodies in his past that served to prove his point.

"I have to go," he said, and before she could say anything else, he ended the call.

Charlie was waiting in the room when Lindsay entered from the bathroom.

Charlie patted on the mattress. "Come and talk to me. I'm so happy you're here. I just wish it was under different circumstances."

Lindsay climbed into bed. "I've spoken to Blake…"

Charlie's eyes widened and she interrupted her. "You've spoken to Blake? I thought you didn't like him and now it's Blake this and Blake that. He's moved in with you and he's kissed you—whatever is going on?"

"There is nothing going on. It's a weird situation. He was worried. I should've told him I was coming here…

"Mmmm." Charlie grinned. "All very interesting observations, but none which explain Blake kissing you, however."

Lindsay shrugged. She had no idea how to answer Charlie—best to steer the subject in another direction. "He's spoken to the policeman from Livingston who arrived on the scene after Mark rammed into us this morning."

"And?"

"And nothing. Mark seems to be able to disappear every time."

"But that's ridiculous. First, he sent someone to do his dirty work for him, and when that didn't work, he came himself. And nobody can catch him?"

"That seems to be the case."

"Well, while you're here, you don't have to worry," Charlie said. "We're not leaving you alone for a minute. And as I've told you before, I've been waiting for Mark-bloody-Taylor for two years."

But Lindsay didn't want to talk about Mark. She had

another question. "Do you know what Blake used to do?"

Charlie shook her head. "Logan isn't talking. He says if Blake wants us to know, he'll tell us. So, you and Blake...?"

"There is no Blake and me, I promise you."

"And the kiss?" Charlie asked again.

Lindsay opened her mouth and closed it again. This was her sister. "He says he's worried about me."

"And? You like kissing Blake?"

Grinning, Lindsay sighed. "I do. But..."

Charlie leaned forward and patted her arm. "There doesn't always have to be a 'but.'"

Lindsay threw her hands in the air. "I don't know if I can trust my own feelings after Mark and Blake... Well, one minute he kisses me, flirts with me, and then he just clams up."

Charlie's eyes widened. "Flirts with you? This is the first time I've heard about flirting. Come on, I need details."

"He phoned just now. And we were flirting—I guess you could call it that—until he said he had to go and then he put the phone down."

Smiling, Charlie got up and gave her a hug. "It sounds to me he's running scared, something men tend to do before they realize they don't want to go anywhere. Logan may be right, after all."

"What do you mean?" Lindsay asked Charlie as her sister walked towards the door.

"We may just have another wedding before Christmas." Charlie laughed over her shoulder before she left the room.

Lindsay's phone bleeped. Another message from Blake. *Hope you can sleep tonight.*

Worry, or something else? She stared at the message for a long time before she started typing.

Are you still on my bed?

She immediately wanted to delete the message, but the

two blue marks indicated he'd already read it. She waited. Her phone bleeped.

No.

The man was driving her insane.

So where are you? Back at your place?

She waited and waited. And just before she put her phone down, it lit up again. Another message from Blake.

In your bed.

Her breath left her body in one swoosh. Oh, my. How was she supposed to sleep, knowing he was in her bed? Her message had only one word.

Why?

Minutes later, there was another message.

What do you put in the perfume you wear?

What kind of a question was that?

Lavender and ylang-ylang.

She waited. Why would he want to know that? In the next heartbeat, she had her answer.

Your pillow has the same smell

She stared at the words for a long time before she sent her message.

Miss you too

The minute she'd sent it, she wished she hadn't. But the two blue marks appeared—he'd seen her words. No taking back what she'd said.

Three dots appeared, disappeared again. She waited. Finally.

I prefer the French version. Goodnight.

French version? Of what? What a weird message. And the "goodnight" obviously meant he was done sending messages.

She put her phone down, switched off the light, and pulled the blanket over her. Everyone else in the apartment was probably already in bed. The only sound was the throb of city life far away.

Nights in Alisson were quiet. She'd had to get used to that after she and Charlie had moved there from the bustling city of Johannesburg in South Africa.

Turning on her side, she closed her eyes. French version. French version of what? He'd sent her a message about her scent; she'd decided it meant he missed her. That was why she'd sent her message, but obviously he'd meant something different or… Thoughts collided and her heart did a double flip.

Quickly, she switched on the light and picked up her phone. Surely Google would know how to translate "I miss you" to French.

Minutes later she stared at the small screen. *Tu me manques.* She wouldn't know how to pronounce the French words, but the direct translation made her heart sigh: *You are missing from me.*

Long after she'd switched off the light again, she found herself still smiling.

CHAPTER 10

Thursday afternoon, Lindsay left a meeting she'd just had with a new oil supplier, a relieved smile on her face. She'd seen quite a number of suppliers over the last two days but this one ticked all the boxes. They had their own organic farmlands and they set the standard for farming and distilling essential oils. The oils they produced were pure, derived naturally through a specific program. She also liked their business ideas—from sustainably sourcing rare botanicals to uplifting local communities, to going above and beyond in complying with local environmental rules.

It was so enriching to be talking about the wonders of essential oils with people who were as excited as she was about the product. And the added bonus? It took her mind away from constantly worrying about what Mark was planning next.

And of course, it kept her from checking her phone for messages from Blake at all hours of the day or night. Since Sunday evening, she hadn't heard from him again. Not that she'd wanted to...

Okay, so not true. She should at least be honest with herself. She'd wanted to hear from him, wanted to know how he'd slept in her bed. Had he been thinking about her? Did he still miss her? And she wanted to tell him how special she thought the French version of "I miss you" was. She'd picked up her phone so many times to tell him, but every time she'd put it away again. If he'd wanted to talk to her, he'd have texted or phoned.

And she also knew flirting with Blake would only lead to heartache. The last thing she should do at this point in her life was fall for someone who so obviously wasn't interested in anything permanent.

Checking her watch, she hastened towards the exit of the building. Charlie should be waiting for her outside. Logan was treating them all to another scrumptious lunch—he'd promised this morning. Over the past few days, her sister hadn't let her out of her sight.

As she stepped out of the building, she saw Logan's car. Charlie was standing beside the vehicle and the moment she saw her, she waved. But something was wrong. She could see it on her sister's face.

"What happened?" she asked as she neared the car.

Charlie gave her a quick hug. "Hi, Linds. Come on, get in the car. We'll talk on the way."

She'd expected to see Eleanor, Brooke, and Connor in the car, but there was no sign of them.

"What happened?" she asked again, her voice not quite steady. Whatever it was, Mark had something to do with it, she just knew it.

Charlie pulled out of the parking space into the traffic. "Everything is okay, nobody was hurt but…Blake has just phoned me. There was a fire in your shop and…"

Lindsay heard the words, but they didn't make sense. Fire. In the shop.

"Blake will be waiting for you at the airport in Bozeman. The rest of us will be back tomorrow. I feel so bad to let you go back by yourself, but Eleanor and Brooke took Connor to the zoo, and Logan is in the middle of—"

Lindsay quickly touched Charlie's arm. She'd disrupted everyone enough over the past few days. "I'll be fine." She shut out everything else and cleared her head. *Think. First things first.* She had to fly back to Bozeman today. "I have to book a plane ticket…"

"Check your phone—Blake said he'd get it and send you the details."

Lindsay opened her emails and there it was—she was checked in already with an electronic boarding pass. The surge of adrenaline left her, leaving her feeling drained. Of course, she would already have her ticket. This was what Blake was good at. He fixed things. "The fire—when did it happen?"

"Apparently late morning. Lilly had been on lunch, and when she returned, she smelled smoke. The fire started in your studio, and fortunately, because Lilly immediately phoned Alisson's Fire and Rescue squad and Blake was close by, it didn't spread. But…I'm sorry, Linds, but it sounds as if your studio is ruined."

"And just when I've finally discovered the right suppliers," Lindsay said, dumbfounded.

"Let's be positive." Charlie briefly touched Lindsay's hand. "You've been talking about expanding your studio for such a long time. Remember we have insurance—for the building and the contents. I'll contact them and get the ball rolling. You may finally be able to get your dream studio. I know it's not easy, but try and see this as a blessing in disguise."

"The fire…it's Mark," Lindsay said. "I'm sure of it."

"It may be. But it could also be faulty electrical wiring. Remember, it's an old building. Let's first find out what the Fire and Rescue people have to say."

They drove to the airport in silence. Lindsay felt like bursting into tears, but she swallowed the lump in her throat. Upsetting Charlie was the last thing she wanted to do.

Blake was at the airport, talking on his phone to the fire chief when Lindsay's plane landed. He kept an eye on the plane as he spoke. "So you're sure it was arson?"

"We have to wait for the investigators to finalize their report before I can make an official statement, but there were indications it was arson. For instance, we found two clear points of origin, one of the things that usually suggests the fire has been set deliberately. But I'll keep you posted."

"Thanks, Chief—I appreciate your call."

They finished the call just as passengers began to disembark from the plane. Blake put his phone away and walked to arrivals to wait for Lindsay.

He scanned the area while waiting, but he didn't see anyone resembling Taylor. There was no doubt in his mind Taylor was behind the fire in Lindsay's studio—a sure way to get Lindsay to return to Alisson. Taylor seemed to be always two steps ahead, and he would've checked flights to Bozeman today and would probably know exactly when Lindsay would be arriving.

It was just after five, the sun had set, and by the time they'd be on the road to Alisson, it would be dark. Earlier he'd also spoken to Jim, the chief of police in Livingston who'd helped them on Sunday. Jim had agreed to check cars driving through Livingston, at least until Blake and Lindsay were safely back in Alisson.

Taylor's actions were escalating, one of the reasons Blake was glad Lindsay was coming home. Taylor was waiting to strike again, he could feel it, and he wanted her close to him when that happened.

Passengers were finally coming through the doors. His heart kicked against his ribs. Any minute now, he'd see her again. And there she was, helping an older woman with her cart. He exhaled slowly. Typical Lindsay. A nurturer. Always giving a helping hand. He remembered the scene in her shop when she took her customer to the mirror, making her feel good about herself.

Another couple rushed forward to help Lindsay and they took the cart from her. They were obviously here to pick up the older woman. As they left, Lindsay looked up and caught his eye. She was clutching her bag, looking beautiful and a little apprehensive.

His feet finally listened to the messages from his brain and he moved forward. For the life of him, at this moment, he couldn't remember any of the reasons why he hadn't talked to her or texted her again after Sunday. At the time, he'd thought he was doing the right thing. Now it sounded ridiculous.

She was also moving towards him, and within seconds, he was right in front of her. With a soft curse, he pulled her close and buried his face in her hair, drinking in her presence, her softness, her scent.

Lindsay clung to Blake. She had no idea what his hug meant, if it meant anything at all, but for the first time since she'd heard about the fire, her shoulders relaxed slightly.

"Thank you for picking me up," she said softly, and pulled out of his arms. If she stayed there a minute longer, she might never want to leave.

"Of course," he said and took her suitcase. "Do you need anything from the store before we leave?"

"Maybe milk and bread…"

But he was shaking his head before she'd finished. "I've bought the necessary; we should be okay for a few days."

She was irked because, while she was nearly hyperventilating after the hug, he seemed totally unaffected by it, and to add to her irritation, he'd again done things she could do herself.

Lifting her chin, she grabbed her suitcase from him. "It has wheels. I can easily pull it myself. There was a fire in my shop. That doesn't mean I'm helpless all of a sudden." And she took off, dragging her suitcase behind her. Seconds later, she stopped. She had no idea where Blake had parked.

He took her hand. "This way," he said gravely but his eyes were laughing at her.

As they walked towards the parking area, she sighed, feeling slightly foolish. "I didn't mean to snap, but you do have a tendency to take over. I've been doing things on my own for quite some time now."

He didn't say anything, just made way for them through the throng of people walking in all directions.

She looked at him but he ignored her and simply kept walking. "I probably owe you quite a lot of money by now. Please let me know what how much I owe you for the plane ticket and everything you've bought for the house," she said.

But instead of answering her, he laced his fingers with hers and kept on walking. They were getting on an escalator, and she pulled her hand out of his to lift her suitcase with two hands.

Again, without saying a word, he picked up her suitcase and took her hand again.

"Seriously, Blake…" she began hotly, but they were at the top of the escalator, and again ignoring her remark, he lengthened his stride as they began walking again.

They reached his car minutes later.

Miffed, she walked to the passenger side. "I could easily have asked Lilly to pick me up. It's quite clear you don't want to be here…"

He was there before her and opened the car door. "And I can open my own damn door," she muttered as she got in.

Pressing his lips tightly together, he closed the door and walked over to the driver's side. Within seconds, he was behind the wheel and started the car.

"Okay, you don't want to talk? Fine by me…"

Cursing under his breath, he turned to her.

"You do know you talk way too damn much, don't you?"

Indignantly, she inhaled, but before she had time to say anything, his hand snaked around her neck and he pulled her closer. She just had time to see his eyes flash before his lips claimed hers in a searing kiss.

Stars exploded behind her eyes and she grabbed hold of his arms. His mouth was warm, urgent, ravaging hers, while his beard against her skin reminded her of the previous time he'd kissed her.

For a moment she was so stunned, she couldn't react, but her body had no problem and responded with joy. Before she could properly process what was happening, her blood had heated to boiling point, her breasts felt heavy, and she was very glad she was sitting down. Standing would definitely have been a problem.

Quite content and shamelessly eager, her tongue met his, and he deepened the kiss. *Oh. My. Word.* Nobody, but nobody had ever kissed her like this before.

He lifted his head, his breath warm on her face, if a little uneven. With an oath, he turned to the front and quickly pulled out of the parking lot. "I'm sorry…I shouldn't have done that. I'm…I have to protect you and I can't do that when I…we…kiss."

Blindly, she stared out of the window—speaking was impossible. Outside, it was dark already and bright lights flashed past her. She touched her lips and closed her eyes. What the man could do to her with just a kiss…

You are missing from me. He'd just kissed her as if he'd really meant the text he'd sent her last Sunday. But then she hadn't heard from him again, but at the airport he'd first hugged her and then kissed her—what did it mean? Did it mean anything?

Swallowing a groan, she inhaled deeply. This was all very temporary, she shouldn't forget that.

As she'd seen on Sunday already, Blake was a good

driver and he deftly maneuvered the car in the traffic. Turning her head slightly, she looked at his hands on the steering wheel. He had beautiful hands. Big. Long fingers. And oh boy, did he know what to do with those hands.

Heat crawled up her neck and she closed her eyes again. Oh, my goodness. She was nearly hyperventilating merely looking at his hands—seriously, she was twenty-six, not sixteen.

Minutes later, they were on the interstate and the traffic was slightly better. He put the radio on, reached out, took her hand, and kept both their hands on his leg.

"The fire in your shop was probably Taylor's way of making sure you return to Alisson. He seems to be two steps ahead all the time, and I'm frustrated. Don't ask me why, but I need to do something, even if it's only to buy milk and bread. And I know I have no right, but at this moment I simply have to touch you." And to her utter astonishment, he lifted her hand and pressed his mouth against her fingers.

"Blake…"

He gave a cheeky grin. "On the bright side—I've discovered the perfect way to shut you up." He chuckled.

She inhaled, ready to explode, but then the realization of how totally she'd overreacted over something trivial really dawned on her. Sheepishly, she smiled at him. "I overreacted and I'm sorry about that, but I do want to pay you back, okay?"

"I'm staying at your house for free, so the least I could do is buy food now and again."

"Having to look after me can't be what you want to be doing with your time…" she began, but he turned his head and the heat in his eyes promptly dried up her words.

He didn't say anything, just laced his fingers with hers. Heat spread through her insides. *Oh, my goodness.*

"Tell me what you know about the fire," she got out. She was supposed to be upset, freaked out, and angry, but look at her. She was nearly salivating because a man had kissed her.

But oh, what a kiss.

And now they were driving back to her house. Where they'd be alone for the rest of the night. She rolled the window down a bit. Icy-cold air hit her hot face, and she closed the window again.

"Too hot?" Blake asked and fiddled with the console of the car. Cooler air filled the car.

She glanced at him. His eyes were on the road, but the corner of his mouth was turned upwards ever so slightly.

"It's hot in the car," she said.

Again, he lifted her hand and kissed her fingers.

"Not helping," she whispered.

"I know. Fortunately, I'm sitting down," he said.

Without any conscious decision on her part, her eyes dropped to his lap.

"Yeah, it's hot in the car." He grinned. He'd obviously seen her noticing his desire.

She tried to pull her hand from his, but he glanced at her. "Don't, please? Told you I need to touch you."

Slowly she exhaled. It was time to talk about this. "It's... Our reactions are only because of the weird situation we're in. You know that, don't you? It's quite normal for two people thrown together in such a tense situation to...well, maybe, develop feelings for... To develop feelings. But it's not real; it's only because of the circumstances. Once Mark is caught, you will disappear, as you tend to do, and life will return to normal."

He didn't answer, just gave her another enigmatic look. The next minute, he bent forward and turned the volume up. "Isn't this the song you danced to the other day? 'Crazy Beautiful'—is that the title?"

"Yeah, it is. But I wouldn't have thought you listen to country music." She grinned.

"I don't usually, but since I've seen you dancing to the tune, I've heard it again a few times."

...*Beautiful to me*, the singer crooned.

"Beautiful to me," Blake murmured the words, glancing at her.

She inhaled shakily. What the man could do to her with just a look. *Talk*. She should talk. The fire. There were still so many unanswered questions. That was what they should be talking about. "Tell me about the fire, please? The shop—any damage there?" she asked.

"No damage in the shop, fortunately. The door to the studio probably needs to be replaced—you'll have to see. But the smell will be bad for a couple of days." He then told her about his conversation with the fire chief.

"So, it was definitely arson?" she asked.

"They're waiting for the official report, but that's what it looks like, yes."

"The studio—is it bad?"

"You should prepare yourself for the worst. It's a mess. What the fire hadn't destroyed, the water probably did. There may be some jars you could salvage, but I doubt it."

Lindsay had to swallow a few times to get rid of the lump in her throat. She wanted to stamp her feet and shout out her frustration, but it wasn't going to help anyone. Nor was crying going to achieve anything. Charlie had mentioned the insurance, the possibility of planning the studio she wanted.

By the time they drove into Alisson, she'd planned a whole new studio in her head.

CHAPTER 11

Blake parked his car next to Lindsay's house. By now, many more houses in the street had Christmas decorations and lights and they were a welcoming sight.

Before he could even get out of the car, she'd already jumped out, battle ready, as he could see in the porch light he'd switched on before he'd left earlier that day. For the last half an hour, she'd been quiet, chewing her lower lip, a clear indication she was thinking and probably worrying. And he hated that. Hated that she didn't share with him what was bothering her.

But it was better than listening to her telling him that what he was feeling wasn't real. Damn it, he shouldn't have told her he missed her—it didn't matter what language he'd used. And he had no right to flirt with her, damn it again.

He knew all too well how feelings could develop in tense situations. That was why what he felt when Lindsay was around, scared the living daylights out of him—he'd never felt like this before.

Still scolding himself, he took her suitcase out of the trunk of the car. And even before he'd closed it again, she'd taken her suitcase and was walking up the stairs.

Cussing underneath his breath, he walked into the street to scan the area. This woman would be the death of him yet.

He wasn't sure whether he wanted to throttle her, or kiss her senseless. And because the latter sounded way too enticing, his best course of action would be to go to bed as soon as he'd checked the doors and windows. But he was hungry and she also hadn't eaten yet. Food had been the last thing on his mind when he'd left for Bozeman. There was bread and cheese, though...

The bright lights of a car approached. His hand went for his gun under his jacket, and he quickly moved back to the house, closer to Lindsay, who was still in front of the door. But when the car turned into the driveway, he saw it was Lilly, Lindsay's assistant at the shop. She jumped out with a casserole in her hand.

"Food!" Lilly called out as she walked closer. "Charlie phoned and asked me to pick up something from the deli—this is their delicious chicken pie."

"Sounds perfect." Lindsay smiled as she walked towards Lilly. "Thanks for all you've done today. If you hadn't been in the shop, it could've been so much worse. I'm so grateful you phoned the Fire and Rescue squad."

"And Blake—he was there within minutes." Lilly smiled. "I just wish I could have done more. I'm so sorry about your studio, Linds." Lilly gave Lindsay a hug. "But Eleanor has already organized for everyone—even though she's still in Seattle—to come and help with the clean-up. Apparently, they'll be returning with Charlie and Logan tomorrow." She turned to Blake. "Do you think the fire department and the police have finished with their investigation?"

"I think so, but they're still waiting on a final report. We should know more by tomorrow," he said.

Lindsay hugged her assistant again. "That is so sweet, Lilly, but I'm not sure whether we can do any cleaning up right away. Charlie was going to contact the insurance people—I suppose they'll need to send someone to assess the damage, as well. The good news is that Charlie thinks we can use the insurance money to make the studio bigger, so it's not all bad news. The cleaning up should wait until I know more." She looked at Blake before she continued. "But I do want to open the shop tomorrow."

Blake gnashed his teeth. "I told you, I don't think that's a good idea. The smell of smoke has been bad. Lilly, tell her."

"I've kept the windows open for most of the day, and I had a few diffusers going, Lindsay—that helped," Lilly said.

Exasperated, Blake looked at Lindsay. "And you do remember there's a madman out there, intent on hurting you?"

Lindsay's chin lifted ever so slightly. Blake swallowed his sigh. Of course, she wouldn't agree with anything he had to say. "There are people around on Saturdays. Lilly will be there, as well."

Lilly winked at Blake before she turned back to Lindsay. "Well, there will be people to help you tomorrow, whether you like it or not."

"Thanks, Lilly, but seriously…" Lindsay began, but Lilly stopped her with another hug.

"By this time, you should know this is how we do things in Alisson, Montana," Lilly teased.

"Thank you." Lindsay sniffled and looked for a tissue in her pockets. "But don't you want to come in? There should be wine…"

"Another time. I have a date!"

They waited on the porch and waved as she drove off. With a soft sniff, Lindsay turned away, her shoulders slumped ever so slightly. He wanted to pick her up, tell her everything would be okay, but better than most, he knew it wouldn't be true.

"I've bought wine…" he began, and she turned around to face him, her chin already in the air. "And before you say anything," he quickly said before she could interrupt,

"I've finished the rest of your wine."

"But there were quite a few bottles left," she exclaimed.

"Well," he said, brushing past her to get to the kitchen, "you were gone for four days."

"What does that have to do with anything?"

He glanced at her. "You really have to ask me that?"

"Yes, I don't see what the one thing…"

He turned and faced her. "I slept in your bed. You weren't here and I've…"

He didn't have to finish the sentence. A soft gasp indicated she knew what he was going to say.

"Don't ask questions you know the answers to. I'll heat the pie, you get the plates," he muttered, not looking at her again. He shouldn't touch her. Because if he did, he wouldn't be able to stop.

"What about a salad?" she asked.

"Sounds fine." He knew he sounded short and rude, but rather that than doing what all his instincts were urging him to do: pick her up, take her upstairs, and make love to her for the rest of the night.

Lindsay made a salad. The simple task took longer than usual; her hands weren't very steady. He'd missed her—was that what he was he was going to say?

Oh, my goodness. How was she supposed to make a salad and not cut herself after seeing the light in those chocolate brown eyes? Strange currents in the kitchen were making her flustered and excited and nervous—all at the same time. But by some miracle, by the time the microwave oven pinged, indicating the pie was hot, the salad was ready, too.

Blake poured them each a glass of wine before he sat down opposite her.

"Tell me about your plans for selling your oils online."

She was taking a sip of wine and looked at him over the rim of the glass. "You're not really interested in oils and creams, are you?"

He looked up. "It's something to talk about."

"Why don't you rather tell me about yourself? You've mentioned you grew up in the system. What did you do after school? Did you go to college? And what was your previous job? The one you still seem to be involved in. You know just about everything about me, but I don't know anything about you."

Lifting his glass, he took a sip of his wine. "Not much to tell. Boring story. I was in the system until Miss Betty O'Hara saved my sorry ass. When she died, I joined the army. Studied through them, and well, that's about it."

He'd used about a minute to sum up his life's story, but because she knew him by now, she could sense the world of hurt behind his words. Her heart was breaking for the little boy who hadn't had a home.

"Don't look at me like that; my life is better than most," he said. "Tell me about your parents. Charlie mentioned at some point they'd died in an accident?"

She nodded and briefly told him about the accident in which her parents had been killed and Charlie had been injured. "And it was during that time I met Mark."

He nodded. "You were vulnerable—he took advantage of that."

"By the time I realized his behavior was abusive, he'd stripped me of my self-confidence. I was at a point where I was agreeing with him how stupid I was—a word he often used. He didn't like my friends or my sister, so at the time, I hadn't seen them for over a year."

"But you managed to walk away," Blake said, reaching out over the table to pick up her hand. "That was a very brave thing to do."

She shook her head, looking at their entwined fingers. "I didn't feel very brave. But Charlie was great."

"So are you. You're anything but stupid. Stubborn, ornery, difficult, yes, but not stupid." He grinned and dropped her hand. He got up. "Why don't you go up to bed? I'll clean up here and make sure everything is locked."

"Ornery? Stubborn, and what was it? Oh, yes, difficult? No wonder you're still single, if those are the lines you use."

He turned his back on her. "Lindsay…please go to bed."

"I'll help," she said, and got up.

"It's better if you don't."

She ignored him and picked up her plate. But before she could move, he'd stepped closer and was right in front of her. His eyes were slits, his teeth clenched together. "Please leave." He tried to take the plate from her but she wouldn't let go.

"Seriously, Blake, I can help clean the kitchen…" But that was as far as she got.

He swooped down and captured her lips with his before her next breath. This time, fireworks went off behind her eyelids, hot lava exploded inside her, and she let go of the plate so that she could touch him.

But he'd already lifted his head and had the plate in his hand. "Thank you," he said and put the plate down on the table. "Now, please, beautiful, go up to your room before I pick you up, take you to my bed, and make love to you until neither of us can think straight."

The words conjured up such a vivid picture of their entwined bodies, a gasp slipped out before she could stop it.

His eyes darkened and he inhaled shakily. "Like you've said, this is not a normal situation—and that's why I think it's best if you go to bed and let me finish here."

She turned around and walked out of the kitchen.

Beautiful. He'd called her beautiful. The way he'd said it, the look in his eyes… Whaaa! She grabbed her bag and raced up the stairs. No meditation or diffuser were going to help her sleep tonight.

CHAPTER 12

By the time two o'clock rolled by, Lindsay was still wide awake. The fire Blake had lit inside of her earlier with his second kiss was still smoldering, had been for the last few hours. And nothing she'd tried so far could calm her busy brain, temper her wayward thoughts, or extinguish the flames threatening to engulf her.

Maybe a cup of tea would help, but lying here, fantasizing about Blake's naked torso, was definitely not sleep-inducing.

She got up without switching on the lights and grabbed her laptop, a pad, and pencil. There were things to do—she could write down all the ideas she had for her new studio and maybe try and make a sketch of what she'd like, more or less.

In her pajamas and only socks on her feet, she slipped out of her bedroom, tiptoed past Blake's door, and jogged down the stairs. She switched on the light and put her laptop and pad on the counter before she put water in the kettle. As she turned around to go back to her computer, a movement at the door made her look up.

Blake was standing there. Without a shirt. He'd obviously quickly put on a pair of jeans, but it wasn't buttoned up.

And he'd shaved. No beard.

Those smoldering embers deep within her caught fire; her breath hitched in her throat as her eyes took on a life of their own and scanned down his body. Lean lines, rippling muscles and...

"What are you doing?" His voice was gravel.

What was she doing? She had absolutely no idea.

"Lindsay..."

She looked up. With his eyes on her, his teeth clenched, he was moving closer to her.

"I...I couldn't sleep," she got out.

"Neither could I."

"You've shaved. Why?" she whispered as her eyes dropped to the magnificent six-pack right in front of her eyes. Totally unprompted, her hands lifted and spread out over his upper body. His flesh was hot, his heart hammering away under her fingers. "I'm making tea," she whispered as her hands boldly glided over hard muscles and supple lines.

Groaning, he caught her hands and pulled her close. "This is a very bad idea. I can't give you what you need."

"And what is that?" she asked, but she wasn't really paying any attention to what he was saying. Her eyes were glued on his magnificent chest.

"I can't promise you forever."

She raised her eyes. "I haven't asked you for that now, have I?" she muttered, but her attention was wandering again. Her hands were still in his, but the rippling muscles were right in front of her mouth. So what was a girl to do but have a taste?

As her lips encountered warm skin, he cussed softly and lifted her chin. His eyes were stormy, desire lurking in their depths. "Damn it, Lindsay, I'm supposed to protect you..."

But she didn't want to listen to any more reasons why she couldn't be with him. She nodded. "So if I'm with you,

I'll be safe. Win-win." And she bent her head again and continued her exploration of warm skin and rock-hard muscles.

Barking out a laugh, he picked her up. "Win-win? You'll be the death of me yet, beautiful."

Her hands explored his broad back while her mouth moved up his neck. Tomorrow, there would be time to scold herself and be appalled at the way she'd more or less jumped his bones, but that would be tomorrow. At this moment, there was no other place she wanted to be than right here in Blake's arms.

He walked straight to her room and gently put her down on the bed. "You know how many times I've imagined being here on this damn bed with you, like this?" he got out as he stared down at her.

She lifted herself on her elbows and looked up at him. The top few buttons of her pajama top had become undone again, leaving one of her breasts bare. Desire literally knocked his breath out and when his knees buckled, he fell down beside her on the bed.

"You're so, so beautiful," he got out, his fingers quickly opening the rest of the buttons so that he could see more of her. "Look at you," he whispered, tracing the lines of her generous curves with unsteady fingers.

"I have to warn you, I'm not very good at this," she said, softly trailing her fingers over his chest.

If he ever got hold of Mark Taylor, he'd find it very difficult not to ram a fist down the man's throat. The damn bastard had her believing she was useless as a woman.

He pressed a soft kiss against her forehead. He didn't have the words to tell her exactly how amazing she was, but he could show her.

"You make me ache for you," he whispered before his lips brushed over her silky skin to capture her lips. Her mouth was warm, moist, and he nearly came undone right there and then. To rein himself in, he moved away from her mouth, pressing kisses all over her face down to the soft spot behind her ear, down her long neck. But instead of calming him down, the sounds coming from her throat, the touch of her hands on his shoulders, and the movement of her body beneath his touch, sent the blood pounding through his body, making his heart gallop at an alarming rate.

"You've asked me why I've shaved. This was what I was thinking about when I got rid of the beard," he muttered before his mouth finally clamped down on one rock-hard nipple. She arched her back, and sobbing out his name, her fingers slid through his hair, egging him on.

Taking his time, he teased and fondled and caressed her breasts, putting everything he was feeling into giving her as much pleasure as he could. When a long, deep moan escaped from her throat, he pushed her pajama bottoms down so that he could continue to savor the silkiness of her skin.

Her flesh heated, quivered under his onslaught; her movements became restless while she dug her nails into his back as his hand found and skimmed down her bared hip. Soft skin. Like petals. Exquisite. But it wasn't enough. Not nearly. He wanted more.

"I want to see all of you." He ground out the words, tugging the pajama bottoms farther down.

She helped him, shrugged off her top, and kicked the bottoms to the side while her hands stroked his chest, driving him wild. One small hand fluttered down, tugged at his jeans. "You're still overdressed," she teased.

He loved her smile and if it were up to him, he'd make sure she'd always be smiling. "Happy to oblige." He grinned and quickly got rid of his jeans.

But by the time he lay down next to her again, she was chewing on her lip, looking uncertain once again. The damn bastard had really done a number on her.

Lifting himself on his elbow, he looked down at her. "You're so, so beautiful," he repeated, cupping her breast. "These…" His lips found hers. "Are the holy grail…" He captured her mouth with his. "I cannot tell you how many nights thoughts of these have kept me awake, how many times I've dreamed of touching you like this."

Far away, a dog barked, a car started up, but Lindsay barely registered the sounds. Her whole being was focused on pleasing this man as much as he was pleasing her. And that was a first.

While his mouth devoured hers, his big, strong hands roamed over her body, touching here, caressing there, until her whole being ached from a need so intense, she was afraid she'd go up in flames any minute.

His mouth moved over her face, down her neck, until it once again fastened around a rock-hard nipple that begged to be suckled while those clever hands slid down her body to where she needed him most. And when he finally cupped her, there was no way she could prevent the whimper in her throat from escaping.

Before she could take her next breath, merciless fingers had found her core, tormenting, teasing, and caressing her until a current simply picked her up and relentlessly dragged her to a place where she cascaded over the top.

Blake watched in awe as her body arched up and she called out his name over and over again. In vain he tried to rein himself in, but seeped in her scent, the blood racing through his veins; he simply had to have her.

She was still shuddering when he hoisted himself above her.

Gasping, she opened her eyes, a small smile playing around her lips.

"Look at me?"

"Blake…" Lindsay's breath caught in her throat as her limbs snaked around him.

Her skin was damp from the heat they'd created. The air around them had thickened, making it difficult to breathe. With one thrust he became a part of her, and when her velvet body clamped around him like a glove, his heart tripped.

This was home. This was where he was supposed to be. Like this, with her.

Lindsay's eyes flew open. Something was different. It took her a few seconds to realize she was lying on top of a very hard body. Blake's very sexy six-pack, to be precise. The one that had caused her numerous sleepless nights over the past few months. And that had been before she'd even seen it.

The day was just breaking, which meant it was a little after seven. She had to get up and go to her shop to assess the mess, but for a little while longer she was going to pretend nothing bad could happen today.

Her one hand was lying as if perfectly content on Blake's chest, while the other one was resting on his shoulder. His broad, muscled shoulder.

She turned her face into his chest. Oh, my. What a night. Blake was a very thorough and ingenious lover. The man didn't use many words, but oh, my goodness, his hands could talk.

At the mere thought, her fingers twitched and began to trail a path along the contours of his muscles. Lazily, she watched as her hand glided over his chest and up his arms to where she explored every inch of his broad shoulders.

Something stirred against her lower body and she turned her head. Blake's eyes were mere slits, but glowing. And in seconds, he had her under him and was sliding into her.

"You were missing from me," he whispered as he laced

his fingers with hers and began to move inside her.

Her heart lifted, hovered for a few minutes before it settled back, shuddering. And in that moment, she knew.

She loved this man. With her body, her mind, her soul, her whole being.

And as her back arched up to him, her heart splintered into a million pieces. She could never tell him, though. He'd made it clear he wasn't interested in forever. This was temporary. They both knew it.

CHAPTER 13

Humming, Lindsay switched on the coffee maker. Her whole body was still glowing. It was already after nine, she was going to be so late, but she'd already sent Lilly a text to warn her. For the first time in days, she was hungry. Last night she didn't have an appetite. Well, not for food, anyway.

Blake was still in the shower, where he'd joined her earlier. She put her hands against her hot cheeks. She'd never be able to step into that shower and not remember the many ways Blake had found to take her to new heights of pleasure.

And she loved him. Deeply, fervently, and with everything she was. She hugged herself. Could anyone be this happy? Look at her—all dressed up to seduce him again. In a pair of jeggings—they wouldn't be so difficult to get rid of as jeans—and one of her favorite pink lace tops. With buttons.

There was a sound behind her, and she grinned. "I have to get to the shop. We can't…" In the next instant, a cold hand clamped down around her throat and she froze.

It wasn't Blake who was standing behind her. It was Mark. She could smell him.

She turned around. And yes, it was Mark. He was standing in the doorway, a gun in his hand, snarling.

"Thought the fire would get you here in time. And no use waiting for Lover Boy upstairs to come your rescue; he's still having a shower. Besides, I've locked the door. What I really wanted to do was to shoot him, here, between the eyes," he said, motioning the gun to the point between his eyes. "But then you'd have heard, and I'm tired of chasing after you. It's time for you to come back to me. You know that, right? You were stupid enough to think you can get away from me, but it doesn't work that way. So, come on, sweetheart, before I change my mind and shoot Lover Boy. He still has no idea I'm here, so don't be stupid enough to think he'll come for you."

He pointed the gun at her.

Still grinning, Blake stepped out of the shower and dried himself. Lindsay had just been in the shower with him, but he already missed her. He had nothing to offer her, he knew that, but hopefully, he'd shown her how wonderfully special she was. And for the moment, he could be with her.

Quickly, he slipped on his jeans and pulled a jersey over his head. And froze.

The hair on his neck rose. Something was seriously wrong—he could feel it. As he sprinted towards the bathroom door, he got out his phone. Panic had him nearly dropping it again.

Damn it, where the hell is Lindsay? He had to get to her, he had to make sure she was safe. That was the reason he was here—to protect her. He should've been more vigilant.

And if he hadn't given in to his desires, if he'd done what he was supposed to do, he would've been. But instead, he was making love to Lindsay when he should've been protecting her. And now she might be in danger. *Damn it to hell.*

The door was locked and there was no key. Which meant someone had reached for the key while he was in the shower and he hadn't even registered what was happening. Dread threatened to engulf him. He stormed back to the window in time to see a black SUV drive away. He couldn't tell the make or the plate numbers from this distance. With unsteady fingers, he dialed Jason's number. It was Taylor, his gut was screaming.

His friend picked up on the first ring. "What?"

"He's got her. Black SUV. Phone everyone."

And roaring, he stormed towards the door and kicked it down. Grabbing clothes and his car keys, he raced down the stairs, an ice-cold hand clutching his heart. Getting into his jeans and boots took a few minutes and by the time he was finished dressing, he was hopping mad. With Taylor, but mostly with himself.

What the hell had he been thinking? He could play house with Lindsay while a madman was after her, and nothing would happen? Cursing, he stormed out of the house and got into his car.

He couldn't protect her because damn it, he'd fallen for her. And look what had happened. She'd been taken while he was in the same house with her. He was supposed to protect her, damn it, not fall in love with her.

Love her. Love.

Cursing, he stepped on the pedal. Because he'd lost his focus, she was in danger. This was all on him.

As he sped away from Lindsay's house, Jason called.

"He's trapped. Only problem is, Lindsay is with him."

"What the hell were you thinking?" Mark demanded again and caught her hair in his hand, as he'd regularly done when they were together.

"You're hurting me," she said through clenched teeth.

"That's the idea, you stupid bitch," he snarled, yanking her hair again.

Lindsay was trying to see where they were going, but her eyes were watering from the pain of Mark's cruel grip, making it difficult to ascertain which direction Mark was driving.

Blake was safe; he hadn't been hurt. This thought kept her sane. And he'd find a way to help her—of that she was very sure.

"You're going to pay for putting me through all of this," Mark shouted, and waving his gun around, continued to verbally abuse her in the most vile language.

She tuned out. It wasn't anything she hadn't heard before. He was clearly unstable, even more so than before. But where his words had usually left her numb with fear, she was now angry. Livid, truth be told. For far too long, he had messed up her life. It was time to take it back.

Just then he swore, dropped his hand, and stepped on the brakes. "What the f—"

They were at the crossroads just outside town, she noticed. But a big, white SUV was blocking the exit. And in front of it were two policemen with guns. The one she recognized as Jim from Livingston, but she hadn't seen the other guy before.

Still swearing, Mark put the car in reverse and looked in the rearview mirror. "What the hell?" he roared.

Lindsay quickly turned her head. Two cars were blocking them from behind, as well. Jason's and Blake's.

"Oh, you think Lover Boy can rescue you?" Mark snarled and opened his door. "Let's show him how happy we are, shall we?" Grabbing her arm, he dragged her across the seat and out of the car.

Outside, he brought his arm around her throat, but she instinctively dropped her chin to prevent him from choking her, and she grabbed hold of his wrist with both her hands.

"You want this piece of trash?" Mark bellowed, waving the gun around. "Why don't you come and get her?"

With a grunt, Blake took a step forward, but Jason put a hand on his arm. "Steady now. He wants you all riled up. Now's the time to let your training kick in. Forget that it's Lindsay out there. There is a victim who needs our help."

Feeling helpless, Blake fisted his hands. Jason was so right. Storming towards Lindsay would only put her in more danger. He usually relied on his instincts, his strength, his fists, but now he needed to think clearly.

"She may not realize it, but look at her, she knows what to do," Jason said softly, his gun aimed at Taylor. "You've taught her the basics of self-defense and she's doing it."

And for the first time, Blake noticed Lindsay had dropped her chin and had both her hands around Taylor's wrist, just like he'd showed them in the self-defense classes. Fear was still clutching at his throat, but there was a glimmer of hope. They didn't have much time, though. At this point, Taylor was so busy shouting instructions, he probably hadn't noticed what she was doing.

Taylor's mistake was to think Lindsay was still the helpless woman he could abuse, but the Lindsay Blake loved was stubborn, ornery, difficult, and strong. Even if she didn't know it yet.

Slowly, without taking his eyes off of Taylor and Lindsay, Blake stepped forward and held out his gun. "I'm putting this down. Let Lindsay go." And as he talked, he moved closer to where Taylor and Lindsay were standing.

"Stay away!" Taylor yelled, and pressed the gun against Lindsay's temple.

Ice-cold fury reared up inside of Blake. This had gone on long enough.

"Lindsay," he said, his eyes on Taylor. "You know you're beautiful, don't you? And strong. So strong. And you know exactly what to do now. We've done it—a number of times—and I remember you were the best."

"Shut up!" Taylor screamed, but Blake was looking at Lindsay. Her chin was still down, effectively preventing

Taylor from choking her.

And then she stepped to her right as Blake had taught her, lifted her left hand, and struck Taylor's groin. And as he bent forward in pain, she hit him with her elbow.

By the time Taylor was howling like a banshee, Blake had picked up Lindsay and was walking back to his car with her. Jason and Jim and the other policeman had Taylor on the ground, his hands behind his back.

In awe, Blake looked down at Lindsay and his eyes roamed over her. She was fine, she was breathing, but her whole body was shaking.

He could've prevented the trauma if he'd been more alert. The same way he could've prevented Miss Betty from dying if he'd noticed in time she wasn't feeling well. The same way he should've had Will's back when he'd stormed into that damn building. But he hadn't been there, for either of his friends.

Lindsay hooked her arms around his neck and as she lifted her head to look at him, he saw the bruises around her neck.

Biting off a curse, he gently put her inside the car. "I'll be with you in a moment." And then he turned around and walked back to where Taylor was still yelling and howling.

Jim and Jason and the other policeman had Taylor cuffed. Blake walked right up to him and lifted his hand.

"I'm taking full responsibility for this," he said, but before he could ram his fist down Taylor's throat, as he'd been wanting to do ever since he'd heard what the bastard had done to Lindsay, Jason grabbed his arm.

"Not worth it," he said. "And the last thing Lindsay needs right now is more violence. Take her home." And as Blake slowly dropped his hand, Jason grinned. "He'll get what's coming to him, don't you worry."

Blake glared at Taylor. At least he'd finally shut the hell up. He wanted to hurt the bastard so badly, but Jason was right. Lindsay didn't need to see more violence.

And he should've thought of that, which just proved his point.

He was no good to her; hadn't he known that it all along?

CHAPTER 14

Lindsay was still shaking like a leaf by the time Blake parked in front of the house. She still couldn't believe what had just happened. And that she'd known what to do to get away from Mark. Because of all those self-defense classes she'd taken, because of everything Blake had taught her, she'd reacted instinctively. Her body had known what to do even though she'd been so scared.

She couldn't know she would react the way she'd just done when confronted by Mark again. But because of Blake's training, because he'd always ask her to come forward during the class when he wanted to demonstrate all the ways one could defend oneself, she'd known what to do. And at the time, she'd been so irritated with him for always making her do it.

Blake had taken her hand in his when they'd driven away from the scene, but he hadn't said another word. She looked at him and her heart melted. How she loved this big man with few words. Turning away, she stared blindly out of the window. But he couldn't or wouldn't give her forever. He'd been very clear about that.

There wasn't any reason for him to stay with her any longer; the danger she'd been in, was over. Because of him.

A big hole opened up inside her but she swallowed against the lump forming in her throat.

It was over. They'd caught Mark. Hopefully, she'd never have to see him again. The constant fear he might discover where she lived was something of the past. He'd found her and yes, he'd hurt her again, but it had been the last time.

This time she waited for Blake to walk around the car and open the door for her. She wasn't sure whether she'd be able to stand up straight just yet.

Her phone rang just as Lindsay was getting out of the car.

"It's Charlie," she told Blake. "Have you told them?"

Shaking his head, Blake closed the car door while she answered the call.

"Charlie…"

"We've just heard what happened…" Charlie hiccupped and promptly burst into tears.

"I'm fine, sis, I really am," Lindsay said but her voice wobbled; she couldn't utter another word.

Wordlessly, Blake held out his hand and she handed him her phone. The next minute she could hear Logan's voice over the phone, and Blake pulled her close to him while he answered all of Logan's questions.

She put her arms around Blake's body and leaned against him. While he spoke to Logan, his other hand moved soothingly over her shoulders and back. Safe. She felt so safe with him. Always had.

Minutes later, he ended the call and returned her phone to her. She dropped her arms, feeling lost and cold.

"They're at the airport in Seattle, on their way. They'll let you know when they reach Bozeman."

Her heart dropped to the ground. His tone was distant, his face closed. Then he turned and walked to the front door. She followed him, dread filling her insides with every step that brought them closer to the door.

He was going to leave. She could see it in the way he

held his shoulders, the way he didn't quite meet her eyes.

And she would have to let him go.

"How do you feel?" Blake asked Lindsay while he closed the door behind them.

"Shaken, but I'll be okay," she said, lifting her chin.

He had to smile. He briefly touched her arm. "Yes, you will be. You were impressive out there, Lindsay Wilson, and don't ever let anyone else tell you otherwise. Look…I…"

Shaking her head, she grimaced and looked him in the eye. "Please, no awkward I'm-sorry-but-it's-me-not-you conversation. You did tell me you can't give me forever. And it's fine. I'm fine. I have to get to the shop—"

"I don't think that's a good idea—" he interrupted, but she didn't give him a chance to finish his sentence.

"Well, fortunately, it doesn't matter what you think." She smiled sweetly. "Tea? Coffee? Or probably not. I'm sure you can't wait to get out of here."

"You should have the doctor take a look at your neck," he said.

She nodded.

For long seconds, he looked at her. Even rattled, she was so beautiful, it hurt. Right in front of him was the person he loved. He could simply put out his hand, touch her, and tell her he loved her. And maybe she loved him back; maybe this was his chance of getting the kind of life he'd never thought he could have. She was the one. His soul mate.

He'd never thought he would feel like this about anyone. And then on a perfectly ordinary evening back in June, he'd walked into a bar and there she'd been—all golden and beautiful.

But even before the thoughts settled, he swallowed in defeat—she could do so much better. He'd only bring her heartache and pain, and she'd had enough of those to last her a lifetime.

"I'll just get my stuff," he said curtly and turned away.

Numb, Lindsay walked into the kitchen and sat down on one of the chairs. It was nearly half past ten. Ninety minutes earlier, she'd been making coffee, her body still glowing after the night spent in Blake's arms. She'd been so, so happy. She'd discovered she loved Blake.

At the time, the threat Mark had posed had been the one false note in her otherwise brilliant day. Now he'd been caught, she should be ecstatic, but any minute now, Blake was going to walk out of her house, out of her life, and she had no idea what to do.

She heard him on the stairs and got up. Combing her hair back, she walked out of the kitchen.

He put his bag down and faced her. His eyes were shuttered, the muscle in his cheek working overtime. "I'm sorry."

"Me too," she said and lifted herself on her toes. "One last kiss?"

For a millisecond, she thought he was going to ignore her and walk away, but with a guttural groan, he pulled her close. He shoved his hands into her hair and then his mouth was on hers. She slipped her hands beneath his sweater, eager to touch him. One last time.

Within moments, Blake's skin was hot and her blood was racing through her body, igniting flames in its wake. She was burning up, her body aching to become a part of Blake's.

He swung her around so the wall was behind her back. Lacing his fingers with hers, he pulled her closer still while he continued to ravish her mouth.

But the urge to touch him was so overwhelming, she pulled her hands from his and again found his naked skin under his sweater. But it wasn't enough. Not nearly. Without taking her mouth from his, she began to unbutton her shirt.

He lifted his head, his eye slits. "Damn, Lindsay…" he groaned and before she could blink, he'd pulled her top over her head and his mouth had fastened over her breast.

The roaring in his ears shut out all other sounds. With his mouth feasting on Lindsay's generous breasts, her hands stroking and kneading his already overheated body, he was ready to explode.

His hand slipped below the soft material of her pants, or whatever the hell she was wearing, intent on getting to her heat. She helped him and quickly, she was nearly naked and his jeans were unzipped.

Gulping in some much-needed oxygen, he lifted his head. Her eyes were liquid blue with need, her lips swollen with his kisses. This was how he'd always remember her.

With a grunt, he lifted her and pushed into her. Home. With his eyes on hers, he began to move.

"Look at me," he whispered while a tornado of passion drove them up a steep hill.

And with her name a mantra on his lips, he slipped right over the edge with her, clutching her close to his heart.

By the time Lindsay opened her eyes again, Blake was gone. The only evidence she hadn't dreamed the last hour was the indent of his head on her pillow.

Pressing her face into the pillow, she inhaled his scent. She'd thought he'd left right after they'd just about ravished each other downstairs, but he'd simply picked her up and brought her back to her bed, where they'd made love again.

Made love. Because that was what it was. On her part, at least. She couldn't tell him what was in her heart, but she'd tried to show him with her body.

But it wasn't enough. He didn't want to stay. It was that simple.

Rubbing her arms, she sat upright. Where her heart had been was a huge hole. And her whole body ached with a pain threatening to cut off her oxygen.

She inhaled deeply. But she had been through worse when her parents had died and her sister had been injured. She'd even survived Mark's abuse.

Getting over Blake was simply another heartache on her life's journey. She had a shop to get to, a damaged studio to fix, and a life to live.

She was going to smile and put one foot in front of the other today, even if it killed her.

Her phone rang. It was Charlie. That meant her sister, Logan, Brooke and Eleanor, and Connor were on their way back. She wasn't alone; she was going to be okay.

And maybe next time the local vet asked her on a date, she'd agree. Roger O'Connor was nice enough, quite attractive if you were going for the white-teeth-blond-curl-on-the-forehead type, but there simply wasn't any spark between them, she'd always thought. But maybe if she actually spent time with him, that could change?

She touched her lips. But nobody would ever be able to kiss her the same way Blake could. Aaargh, this wasn't helping.

She answered her phone.

Blake was on the phone to Eric Walker, the chief of the Violent Crime Unit of the FBI, before he'd turned off the street where Lindsay lived. He had to get away from Alisson as soon as possible.

Eric was happy to hear his voice, and yes, he was told, the case was still ongoing and they would welcome his input.

His next call was to Jason.

"You can relax, he's behind bars." Jason answered the

call succinctly.

"Good to know. I'm leaving for Washington and was hoping you could continue with the dojo until the week before Christmas when we close?"

Silence.

"Jason?"

"So you're running away?" Jason finally asked.

"No."

"Sounds like running away to me."

"I spoke to Eric. I'm going to help with a case."

"You do know you don't have to. You don't work for them any longer."

"If you can't continue with classes…" Blake said, ignoring Jason's words.

Jason chuckled. "I think I'm beginning to understand what is going on here. You've gone and fallen in love with Lindsay Wilson and now you're running scared. That's why you're leaving. At least admit the real reason you're bolting."

Blake stopped next to the small house he rented. He'd never planned on staying here, anyway. That was why he hadn't bought any property. Well, except for the building where the dojo was.

Rubbing his face, he switched off his car. "You're right. I…feel something for her, but I always let those I love down, no matter how hard I try not to. And Lindsay's been hurt enough; she doesn't need to add me to her problems."

"And you leaving won't hurt her?" Jason exclaimed. "Have you seen the two of you together? You can't keep your hands to yourself and she lights up whenever you're around."

"Keep an eye on her for me, will you?" Blake asked shortly.

"And what? Let you know when someone else wants to marry her? Because that will happen sooner or later. You realize that, don't you?"

"Thanks for helping out at the dojo," Blake said and ended the call.

Lindsay getting married to someone else. A sharp sword pierced right through his heart. Taking out his phone, he quickly climbed out of his car. There was a plane ticket for him. He was leaving in a couple of hours from Bozeman. There wasn't much time to pack.

Fortunately, he travelled lightly—his motto in life. There was no way he could be a husband, a dad. He wouldn't know how to be one.

Swearing, he opened his front door. Husband. Dad. Not words he'd ever thought would cross his mind. Remember that, he told himself. Remember that.

CHAPTER 15

"Oooh, I can't wait for six o'clock!" Lilly giggled and twirled in the middle of the shop.

Lindsay smiled. It was impossible to stay mad at Lilly. The dear girl hadn't been able to focus on anything today. Well, actually the whole week.

It was the end of the first week of December, the Christmas activities in Allison had begun, and Lilly had her eye on a young fireman. He was all she'd been talking about all week. It was Friday night, and tonight would be the annual Christmas Stroll, one of the many items on the agenda for the coming weeks. Everyone joined in and the festivities usually brought the whole town together.

It had been a busy week and Lilly's absentmindedness was creating all sorts of problems. Charlie had had several double bookings this week, bottles in Lindsay's shop had been placed in strange places, and Lilly had been on her phone most of the time.

"And next weekend is the Snowflake Festival, for three whole days!" Lilly sang as she continued dancing around the shop. "Don't you just love this time of year?"

Behind Lilly's back, Lindsay rolled her eyes. Could they survive another week of Lilly walking on clouds and talking non-stop about her fireman?

Immediately ashamed about her unkind thoughts, Lindsay put a smile on her face. Just because she didn't have any expectations as far as love was concerned, it didn't mean other people wouldn't fall in love. It was the season in which magical things could happen. Just not to her, it seemed.

The door opened and Eleanor strolled in, dressed in red from top to toe. Making a turn, she clapped her hands. "Oh, Lindsay and Lilly, you've outdone yourself this year with decorating your shop—it looks delightful. By far the best Christmas-feeling shop in town."

Lindsay hugged her friend with a real smile. Nobody could stay sad or irritated when Eleanor was around. "I love a winter Christmas. You remember our mother was American and our family often visited Aunt Charlotte here, in Alisson, over Christmas. For us, the snow and the sleighs, the time spent with family, and all things Christmas were pure magic. Christmas in South Africa is so different. To begin with, in December, it's summer in the southern hemisphere. We used to spend Christmas Day on the beach!"

Eleanor shuddered. "That just sounds so wrong. I, for one, am so glad you and your sister have moved here. I'm Christmas shopping today. Next week Brooke and I are going to Bozeman. She got tickets for us to go and see *The Nutcracker*. Both of us love ballet and it will be Connor's first experience."

"Oh, he'll love it!" Lilly exclaimed. "But you'll be back in time for the Snowflake Festival, won't you?"

"Of course. We won't miss that." Eleanor turned back to Lindsay. "Why don't you join us, Lindsay?"

"Thanks, but we're so busy right now." Lindsay smiled. She couldn't conjure up any excitement for anything, and with the mood she was in, she would spoil the outing for everyone.

"Maybe next time, then?" Eleanor smiled. "Is your

brother not supposed to be back in Alisson already?"

"Soon, we hope. He still can't give us an exact date, though." Lindsay nodded. "It'll be so great to have him here and to know he doesn't have to go back again."

"I'm so happy for you. And especially for all the unmarried ladies in town." Eleanor winked.

"I don't know about that," Lindsay replied. "He's not very enamored by the ladies at the moment. Bad break-up."

"Alisson has a way of changing people's minds, you know," Eleanor said. "Who knows? Maybe he'll find the love of his life here."

Smiling, Lindsay shook her head. "Forever the romantic. But unfortunately, ordinary life doesn't always work that way."

Eleanor touched her hand. "It can be if you're brave enough," she said softly before she motioned with her hands. "I'm looking for something for Brooke. The poor girl worked so hard to finish the paintings for her exhibition next year. She wants to spend time with Connor during the school holidays. So I want to get her something special for Christmas. I know she loves your creams."

"Well, come on then, let me show you—I've made a new batch that smells divine."

"And your lovely studio? Any news when they can start rebuilding it?" Eleanor asked as they walked past the door that used to lead to the studio.

"Everything is on track, but they won't begin building before next year. But it's okay. I've converted the one room at home into a temporary studio, so I'm able to mix my creams. What Gavin is going to say about all the smells, I can just imagine."

"Brooke said you showed her the plans and it'll be much bigger than before?"

"Yes, exactly what I've wanted. I'm really looking forward to having more space. Here we are." She picked up a tester jar and opened it. "Try this cream. It leaves your skin glowing. Lovely smells of frankincense, myrrh, and geranium with a little helichrysum in rosehip oil."

Eleanor smelled the cream and rubbed a little onto her hand. "Ooh, I love it. I think I also want one of those. I'm probably beyond redemption, but what the heck, it's Christmas—miracles can happen."

Lindsay smiled but her heart ached. That word again. Miracle. She'd been hoping for a miracle for the past three weeks. Ever since Blake had left, she'd been dreaming about him striding into her shop with his big, lopsided grin. She missed him more with every passing day. It had been three weeks since she'd seen him, made love to him, kissed him. Surely, by now she should be able to not think about him every single minute of every day?

"Have you heard anything from Blake?" Eleanor asked innocently.

Lindsay shook her head as she wrapped the creams for Eleanor. "No, I haven't."

Fortunately, at that moment another customer entered and Eleanor couldn't ask any more questions. Since Blake had left, Eleanor, Brooke, and Charlie had been taking turns asking her whether she'd heard from him. She wished she had a different answer for them, but he was gone; she wasn't going to hear from him ever again.

She hadn't even told her own sister about the night she and Blake had spent together. Or what had happened between them just before he'd walked out of her life. It was still way too painful to talk about him.

She put her hand against her heart. Surely, at some point, the pain would be more bearable?

Later that evening, Lindsay finally locked the door to her shop to join Charlie and Logan, who were waiting for her outside in the street. To everyone's delight, it had been snowing all day.

The street was busy with people scuttling in and out of

shops, children racing around or taking rides with the sled dogs or on wagons.

"Come on, Linds," Charlie called out. "Let's move, it's cold! Once the lights have been turned on, Logan will treat us to a hot dinner."

"That sounds lovely." Lindsay smiled and patted Charlie's tummy. "How's my niece? A little girl, sis—I'm so happy for you."

Charlie's eyes filled up and she hugged Lindsay. "I know. I never thought I'd be pregnant. I still pinch myself every day."

"Do we have a name yet?" Lindsay asked as they joined everyone else who was walking down Main Street."

Charlie looked up at Logan. "It's a secret—we'll share on Christmas Day. I'm so looking forward to having everyone on the ranch. I do hope you and Gavin will also stay with us for a few days?"

"Let's see. Hopefully he'll be here a few days before Christmas."

Charlie sniffled and looked for a tissue in her bag. "I'm going to cry again!" She laughed. "These hormones are really messing with me. But I'm so happy he'll also be close by." She looked past Lindsay's shoulder and smiled. "Hi, Jason."

Lindsay turned around quickly. Since Blake's departure, she hadn't seen or heard from his friend. "Hi, Jason. Nice to see you."

"Join us, Jason, we're on our way to the square to watch the lights being turned on and then we're having dinner." Charlie smiled.

"Thanks, sounds nice." He grinned.

"Hi, Lindsay," another voice called out, and Stacey's red head appeared.

"Hi, Stacey, it's cold, isn't it?" Lindsay greeted her friend and they hugged. "I don't think you've met my sister and her husband? And this is Jason Coleman, also a friend. Everyone, this is Stacey Lawrence, she's doing the website for my shop." She made the introductions before all of them followed the rest of the crowd down Main Street towards the village square.

Charlie began to talk to Stacey, and Lindsay took a deep breath. This was her chance to find out if Jason knew anything about Blake. She cleared her throat and Jason chuckled.

"You want to know how Blake's doing?"

She nodded.

"You could just phone him and find out, you know? That's what I told him."

"You spoke to him?"

"Texted. I get a message from him just about every day. Always with the same question."

Lindsay's heart was just about jumping out of her body.

"And what is that?"

"How's Lindsay?"

"Why doesn't he ask me?" she asked, pressing her lips together.

"That's what I said."

They walked in silence for a few minutes. Seconds later, Jason was the one to clear his throat. "Blake...well, he lost two people close to him in the past and still reckons it was his fault. He doesn't think he has anything to offer you."

Lindsay lifted her chin. She was done asking Blake for anything. "Well, that's very clear then. I..."

"Well, if it isn't the beautiful Lindsay Wilson," a voice drawled close by.

Lindsay sighed but she turned her head and smiled. The local vet was walking behind them, grinning broadly with his very white teeth. "Hi, Roger."

"What about dinner later?" he asked.

"Not tonight." She smiled over her shoulder. "Give me a call after Christmas, won't you?"

Next to her Jason chuckled. "You don't really want to go out with him, do you?"

"He's nice," Lindsay said shortly.

"He smiles all the damn time," Jason said.

"Well, it's better than being taciturn all the time, like some people I know." And she turned and began to ask Stacey about her website. It was hard enough to carry on day by day without Blake; she didn't also want to have to talk about him.

Damn it, she hadn't been looking for love; he was the one who'd insisted on protecting her. So, he'd lost two people close to him and that was his reason for not wanting to be with her? So had she, but she'd been prepared to open her heart to him anyway. What utter nonsense, and if she'd ever have the misfortune of seeing him again, she'd tell him that.

By ten, Lindsay couldn't keep her eyes open, and picked up her bag. "Thanks for the lovely dinner, Logan and Charlie, but I need my beauty sleep.

"It's only ten o'clock," Eleanor cried out. "The night is way too young for you to leave just yet. Besides," she whispered with a wink, "I want to know about you and the vet."

"Mom, seriously," Brooke scolded.

"What? I'd thought she and Blake would hit it off, but both of them are too blind or too stubborn or too whatever. Anyway, life is short. Maybe Roger could be your backup plan."

But Lindsay just smiled and waved to everyone. Charlie got up. "Give me a hug. Are you feeling okay?" she asked.

"Of course. It's just been a busy week."

"Let me walk you to the door," Charlie said. "How are you really? And don't you dare give me another 'I'm fine.' I don't believe you anymore. You're pale, you have circles under your eyes, which tells me you haven't been sleeping properly, and you've stopped smiling."

Lindsay threw up her hands. "What do you want me to say? Mark has been caught; I can't begin to tell you what a relief that has been. I've only now come to realize over the past two years I've constantly been worrying he may show up here in Alisson."

"His mistake was thinking you are still the same woman you were before. I'm so, so proud of the way you handled the whole thing. I'm very glad I didn't have to watch him manhandling you, but you were so brave."

"I'm really okay, sis…" she began, but Charlie shook her head.

"You're miserable and Mark has nothing to do with that. Talk to me." Charlie pulled her to the side. "You haven't been very forthcoming about what really happened between you and Blake, but tell me—did the two of you end up in bed?"

"What does that have to do with anything?" Lindsay asked, blushing.

"As I've mention, you're looking pale, and I've heard you mention more than once you're tired." Charlie grinned. "It's just, when I was so tired, it turned out I was pregnant."

Lindsay stared at Charlie, her mind blank for a moment. Then she laughed. "Don't be silly, I can't be… Besides, it's way too early to know."

Charlie's eyes widened. "Ah. So you did sleep with him?"

Lindsay nodded.

"And how was it? And why haven't you told me? I'm your sister and your BFF!"

"It was really amazing, but it was a one-time thing… Well, okay, twice, but he was very clear about the fact he's not interested in anything more." Lindsay swallowed, her thoughts racing. "But I can't be pregnant…" Shaking her head, she dug out her car keys. "I'll see you tomorrow."

"Linds…"

But panicking, she quickly made her way to the exit. Pregnant? She couldn't be pregnant, could she? As she'd told Lindsay, it was way too early to tell; Blake had left three weeks ago. And besides, Blake had used protection every time, she was sure of it.

Except... She stopped. Except that last time.

It was still snowing lightly. She lifted her face up to the grey sky. Pregnant? With Blake's baby? A little boy with his daddy's serious brown eyes? Something warm opened up inside her, and the heat spread throughout her body.

Her heart aching, she continued to her car. She might be pregnant or she might not be. Whatever the case, she was alone in this. Blake had walked away, remember?

CHAPTER 16

Blake stood next to Eric, looking down at the plans of a building as his boss explained a possible strategy to finally catch the thieves who'd been robbing banks all over the country.

It was Wednesday, the second week in December. The team had been tracking the movements of this gang of bank robbers for the last two months by the time Blake had joined them nearly four weeks ago. Over the last week, they'd finally caught a break when they'd received a tip via the Bank Robbers Mobile App, an application launched by the FBI in 2016, to make it even easier for the public to help law enforcement.

The site and app offered a search tool to find and group robbers by location, a national map that plotted robbery locations, a chronological list of robberies, electronic wanted posters with details on each robber and crime, and a printable version of each poster containing information on how to contact authorities.

They were flying to Chicago tomorrow. Everything had been planned down to the last detail. A technical team would be on standby, with eyes and ears outside and inside the building.

As Eric droned on, Blake tuned out. They'd gone over the details enough times for him to know what needed to be done. The one question he kept asking himself over and over, though, and one he couldn't find an answer to was, why was he here?

He'd resigned. Walked away from this life after Will's untimely and unnecessary death. But when Eric had contacted him months later, he'd immediately agreed to help. He couldn't bring back Will, but he could make sure no one else died, he'd reasoned. There had been an urgent need inside him to try and atone, somehow, for his partner's death.

But, as he'd come to realize, he could never do that, no matter how many times he put himself in danger—something that had only gradually dawned on him over the last week.

And over the last few days, Jason's words were keeping him awake at night. Will shouldn't have stormed into the building without backup. He knew that. And he was finally able to grasp—on some level at least—Will's death hadn't been his fault.

And Miss Betty had been old and ill. The reason why she hadn't told him was because she hadn't wanted him to worry about her.

But his discoveries—realizations—didn't change much, really. He still didn't have anything to offer Lindsay. Oh, he had money. Thanks to Miss Betty's very generous inheritance, he would probably never have to work again, but he'd didn't know the first thing about being part of a family or what a dad was supposed to do.

But damn it, did he miss her. He'd picked up his phone too many times to count, intent on sending her a message, only to put it down again. She needed someone who understood the meaning of family, not someone like him, who had no idea what it meant.

Love. Such a small word. Such a powerful emotion.

"Davidson? Your head in the game, or on some or

woman?" Eric's crisp voice penetrated his thoughts.

"I'm here," he said.

Eric stared at him a moment longer before he scanned the room. "See you at the airport tomorrow morning at seven. Be ready."

As they all left the room, Blake's phone rang. It was Jason. His heart missed a beat. Lindsay.

"What's wrong?" he asked without greeting Jason.

"Depends."

"What are you talking about?"

"On whether you're certain you're not interested in Lindsay," Jason said coolly. "I've been wondering for the past week whether I should tell you."

Blake's heart simply stopped. "Tell me what?"

"It's December. Nearly Christmas, and the good people of Alisson have planned all sorts of entertainment for the next few weeks. And as you know, Lindsay is single, the local vet is single; come to think of that, I'm single..."

Blake gritted his teeth. "I told you to stay away, remember?"

"Ah. So you won't like it if I ask her to the Snowflake Festival this weekend? It's just...there'll be dancing and I..."

"Stay. Away."

"Okay, but just so you know—the vet is just about salivating when he looks at her... I mean, Lindsay is—"

"Don't you dare say another word."

Jason laughed. "Well, my friend, you'll have to make up your mind quickly. If you're not back, the playing field is open!" And with that, he ended the call.

Cursing under his breath, Blake took the elevator. His hands were fisted, he noticed, and tried to relax his fingers, but the mere thought of Lindsay with another man made him see red.

The elevator stopped on the ground floor; he strode towards the doors, ignoring everyone else. He needed some fresh air to clear his head. As he stumbled out of the building in downtown Washington, he turned and looked back at it.

The decade-long plan to build new headquarters for the FBI in the Washington suburbs had been cancelled by the current president three years before. But apparently, there was now funding for a new headquarters project in Huntsville, Alabama; this one wasn't secure enough and was just about crumbling around them.

It was time to renew, time to rethink old ideas and old plans. What worked before wasn't working anymore.

Looking up at the blue sky, he inhaled deeply. Wasn't it time to rethink his own damn life? One of the reasons he'd chosen to open his dojo in Alisson, Montana, when he left the FBI, was because of the fresh air and the particular shade of blue of the Montana sky. So why the hell was he here and not there?

Lindsay. Rubbing his chest, he grimaced. Damn, he loved her. He didn't want to be here; he didn't want to be killed; he wanted to spend whatever time he had left on this earth with her—if she'd have him back—if she would agree to his terms.

He couldn't ever be a husband or father, but he could love her. Maybe that would be enough? He was prepared to grovel and crawl if that was what it would take to convince her to give him a chance.

For the first time since he could remember, he was excited about the future. He had a new plan.

So how could he convince her to let him into her life again? She felt something for him. She wouldn't have let him touch her, otherwise. And he was going to make sure no other damn man was going to put his hands on her.

Turning around, he went back into the building, his tread much lighter.

He'd fly back to Bozeman from Chicago when they'd finished tomorrow night, and surprise Lindsay. He should be in time for whatever-the-hell-the-name-was festival. If anyone would be dancing with her, it would be him. The damn vet could get his own woman.

Thursday night, the tension was palpable in the vehicle as Eric parked a block from the building they were about to enter. They'd arrived in Chicago that morning and since then had made sure everything was in place for their plan.

"Everything okay, Davidson?" Eric asked as they got out of the vehicle. "You're very quiet. I need your head here, with us."

Two other vehicles, carrying the other four agents on the team, stopped behind them.

"I'm here," Blake said, his gun also ready. Why the hell everyone had to talk all the time, he didn't know. He was fine. He didn't really sleep. Or eat. And he couldn't stop thinking about Lindsay, but other than that, he was fine.

The rest of the team hurried closer and Eric barked out last orders. Everyone knew what to do and the technical team was nearby. But as Blake had discovered in the course of his career, you could never predict every little detail. It had been exactly one such surprise that had killed his friend.

It was freezing cold in Chicago, as always. Quietly, they moved closer to the building.

Blake followed Eric down a small alley next to the building. According to the floor plans they'd studied, there should be a door ahead. Slowly, they crept towards it.

Lindsay. Her image flashed before his eyes as it had done numerous times over the last three weeks.

Eric lifted his hand, counted on his fingers from three. Two other team members rammed the door and they were inside. Blake followed silently, aware of the rest of the team behind him.

Suddenly, he stopped. He'd picked up a sound coming from the opposite direction from where they were headed. Something was wrong.

He touched Eric's shoulder and when he turned

around, Blake shook his head, indicating they should stop.

But Eric had smelled victory. He shook off Blake's arm and began to move forward again. Even more alert than before, Blake scanned the area around them. As they proceeded around a corner, a movement out of the corner of his eye had him turning to his right, gun ready.

He caught the flash a millisecond before the sound rang out. "Gun!" he shouted, and jumped in front of Eric without a second thought. The man had kids and a wife.

Chaos broke out but Blake ignored everything else. His eyes were trained on the spot where he'd seen the gun fire. He fired two shots. Someone fell, called out.

Dropping his arm, he looked around for Eric, but a strange numbness was crawling over him. He looked down at his arm. Blood was dripping on the floor. Whose blood? The person he'd shot was way over on the other side.

"Davidson...son of a..."

Blake heard Eric's voice from far away. A blackness threatened to engulf him. Damn, he'd been shot.

Lindsay. He loved her. And he would never get to tell her that; he'd never get to dance with her to that song she liked or make love to her again. They would've made beautiful babies. Two little girls with their mother's clear blue eyes and a boy with dark hair. They'd have a house with fairy lights all around the porch. And a dog. A damn spaniel, of all things.

Lindsay was trying to tell him something. He wanted to hear what she had to say, but he couldn't keep his eyes open.

Lindsay swallowed the lump in her throat. Damn it, she kept wanting to cry over every stupid little thing.

It was Thursday evening and everyone was gathered on the town square, getting the booths ready for the weekend-long Snowflake Festival, which would start tomorrow. She and Lilly were decorating their cubicle. With Lilly's help, she'd made gift packs with her creams and oils, ready to be sold.

All the trees around the big Christmas tree were covered in lights, giving a magical feeling to the whole square.

"Linds!" she heard her sister call, and looked up to see Charlie hurrying closer.

Lindsay smiled. Her sister was literally glowing. Logan was a few steps behind. "Slowly, Charlie…" He laughed and pulled his wife closer for a hug.

Charlie beamed. "How are you?" she asked Lindsay. "Still feeling tired?"

"I…" she began, but someone touched her arm and she turned around. It was Jason.

"Can we talk?" he asked.

Her heart stopped. Something was wrong; she could read it in Jason's somber face. "What's wrong? Has something happened to Blake?"

He hesitated and glanced at Charlie.

"What's happened?" her sister asked and rushed closer.

"I…don't know." She looked up at Jason and her heart stopped. "Blake," she barely got out. "Something happened to Blake. Tell me!"

"Jason?" Logan asked as Charlie grabbed her hand.

"He's been injured…"

Lindsay could see Jason's lips move, but she couldn't make out the rest of his words. Why couldn't she breathe? She tried to focus, but a soft cloud simply picked her up and a blackness engulfed her.

CHAPTER 17

"Linds, sweetie, please breathe," Charlie said for the umpteenth time. "Otherwise, you may pass out again. Not something I want to see again," she teased.

It was Friday afternoon. They were still in the plane, waiting for the doors to open. They'd just arrived at Chicago's O'Hare International Airport after a nearly three-hour flight.

At times like these, she was grateful for her brother-in-law's generosity. They'd flown business class and would be some of the first passengers to leave the plane.

Lindsay nodded, inhaling deeply. She'd had her arms clasped tightly around her body, scared if she let go, she'd fall to pieces. It was still difficult to believe she'd fainted last night. But she'd hardly eaten throughout the day.

To her dismay, there hadn't been any direct flights from Bozeman to Chicago before twelve noon, which meant she had to wait about twenty hours before she could board a plane to get to Blake. Driving to Chicago would've taken even longer.

She hadn't even bothered to go to bed last night; sleep was out of the question. After she'd seen Blake, after she knew he was going to be okay, there'd be enough time to sleep.

He'd been injured. That was all Jason had told them and all she could think about during the long night. She still didn't know how and why he'd been injured. Jason just shrugged when she'd asked. Over the course of the long night, she'd willed herself not to think about worse-case scenarios, but of course, she'd ended up picturing all the worst possible outcomes, driving herself crazy.

She'd stayed on the ranch with Charlie and Logan last night, and they both had insisted on coming with her today. Jason was also with them. It would make things easier to get to Blake, he'd explained.

Jason had phoned several times before they'd boarded the plane in Bozeman, but all she knew for certain at this point was that Blake had been injured. Jason kept giving her vague answers. She was just about ready to shake the big man.

As they entered the airport building, she looked at Jason. "Will you please try again to find out what's going on?"

"We'll be at the hospital in no time," he said, and continued his long strides.

"Come on, sis, we're nearly there." Charlie smiled. You okay?"

"I will be when I see Blake."

"Well, at least now you know." Charlie chuckled.

Irritated, Lindsay glanced at her grinning sister. This was so not the time to find anything funny.

"That you love the guy." Charlie smiled.

And the lump in Lindsay's throat was back. She nodded. "I do. What if I never…?"

"No negative thoughts, remember?" Charlie asked.

They all had only hand luggage and didn't need to wait, but it still took ages to get outside the huge, impressive terminal.

"Here's our ride." Jason grinned and walked towards a black car parked right outside the entrance. "Our former boss when Blake and I worked for the FBI—Eric Walker."

Lindsay stared at Jason and he nodded slightly. So both he and Blake had worked for the FBI? Everything made sense now. Blake's contacts, the way he knew things about her, his long absences.

She focused on the tall, grim man. "But if you're his former boss, how come…?"

"He's helped us in the past on a consultation basis," Eric said.

Also not one for many words. "How's Blake?" she asked.

A very small smile lifted the corners of his mouth. "He'll live. He's a stubborn devil; no bullet is going to stop him."

"Bullet…?" She could literally feel her blood freeze.

"But he's okay," Jason quickly said before she could take another breath. "Tell her, Eric. I left out the part about…well, the bullet."

Eric grimaced. "Oh, sorry. Yes, he's okay. The doctors operated on him last night, and he's already giving the hospital staff hell, but he's okay."

"Operated on him? Why didn't you tell me?" she asked Jason crossly.

He shrugged. "Because of how you're reacting now."

Inhaling sharply, she turned back to Eric. "Please take me to him."

Eric nodded. "Of course. I'm your ride."

She ignored Jason.

Blake was ready to explode. He'd been shot before, damn it. This wasn't his first rodeo. It hurt like hell, but it would get better. Why the hell did he have to stay another night like the doctor insisted?

He'd just received a tray of food. His supper, he was told. It was six o'clock, damn it. Who the hell ate this time of day? Muttering and cursing, he sat up in the bed. He was feeling fine. And he'd be even better if he could get to the airport so that he could get to Lindsay.

As he swung his legs from the bed, the nurse, who'd been giving him hell all day, walked in. A real ball-buster. But this time he was going to ignore her.

"Where do you think you're going?" she asked, hands on hips.

"Home," he said, and got up. It was more difficult than he'd imagined, because the arm they'd operated on was in a sling.

"I'm calling the doctor," she threatened.

"Go ahead," he said, looking around for his clothes. "Where's my stuff?" he asked.

"You don't have stuff," she said smugly, crossing her arms.

"My clothes?" he snarled.

"You were shot. Everything was taken. Now get back into bed or help me—"

"Where's my phone?"

"You can't get your phone," she said.

"I want my phone, dammit to hell!" He was frustrated and in pain; good manners didn't seem to matter at the moment.

"Well, well, what do we have here?" a voice asked from the doorway and when he looked up, Jason was standing there with a broad grin.

"They took my phone," Blake immediately complained. "And I have no clothes. I have to get back to Alisson. It's the damn Snow-of-Whatever-the-Hell Festival and nobody else will be dancing with Lindsay but me!" he bellowed.

"Well, I would suggest you get back into bed." Jason chuckled as he led him back to the bed. "Because I don't think you want Lindsay to see you in this outfit. Really embarrassing, man."

Lindsay's heart was beating so loudly in her chest, she

was certain everyone else could also hear it thundering away.

They'd all heard Blake shouting he wanted his phone. Jason had been a little ahead of her and, smiling at them over his shoulder, had entered Blake room's first. They'd all heard his last words to Blake.

"What the hell do you mean?" Blake shouted.

"I mean…" Jason began pushing him down on the bed.

"Go!" Charlie giggled and pushed her towards the door. Taking a shuddering breath, Lindsay walked into the room.

"I'm here," she said softly, waiting for Blake to look at her.

His head swiveled in her direction, brown eyes met hers, and her heart sighed. He was okay—pale, his hair standing on end, a sling on his arm, but his eyes were warm, he was breathing, he was okay.

"Please tell me you're Lindsay?" someone asked. Lindsay turned her head. A clearly fed-up nurse was looking her up and down.

"She is," grinned Jason.

"Well, thank goodness. This one hasn't stop jabbering about you since they've brought him in. Even unconscious, all he kept repeating was your name. Good luck to you, missy—you've got your work cut out for you." And with a sniff, she stormed out of the room.

Charlie, Logan, and Eric also entered the room, but Blake didn't take his eyes off her. Even when they talked to him, he answered them, but kept looking at her.

"Okay, well. I don't know about the rest of you, but the baby and I need food," Charlie announced.

Logan smiled. "The two of you are always hungry. Come on. Jason? Eric?"

And within seconds, only she and Blake were left in the room.

"I'm so glad you're okay," she got out.

"I can't believe you're here."

"I had to see if you were okay. FBI, huh?"

Smiling, he held out his hand. "Yes, but that's over now. Come here, you're very far away."

She moved forward and he caught her hand, pulling her closer.

Worried, she touched his arm. "What about this?"

"I don't need my arm to kiss you," he said and drew her closer so that she was sitting next to him on the bed. "And I really, really need to kiss you right now." His hands cupped her face. "Do you have any idea how I've missed you?" he murmured before his lips captured hers.

There were so many questions, but there would be time for all of that later. Right now, she was enjoying kissing the man she loved.

When he finally lifted his head, his eyes were molten chocolate. With an unsteady hand, he stroked her face. "I love you. And I want to spend the rest of my life with you. When I was shot, all I could think about was I wasn't going to get the chance to tell you that." And with his lopsided grin, he motioned to the room. "Not the most romantic place to declare one's love, but I'm not waiting any longer. But…"

Lindsay's heart had just begun to soar, when she registered the "but." Of course, there would be a "but." There always was one. This was real life, not a movie.

He inhaled shakily. "I've mentioned Miss Betty before, but I want to tell you about her and Will, then you'll understand why there is a 'but.'" And taking her hand in his, he told her about the woman who had saved him all those years ago when he'd only been twelve.

"She wouldn't give up on me." He smiled. "I tried my usual stunts but she never returned me to the system like the other foster parents did. She kept loving me until I had no choice but to love her back. And then…she died. She didn't tell me she was ill, and for a long time, I blamed myself for not noticing, for not being able to protect her."

"You couldn't have known," Lindsay said.

"I finally realized that. I also couldn't protect Will. He was my partner while I worked for the FBI."

"Tell me about him?" she asked, and listened as he described the friend he'd made after he'd joined the FBI.

"We were more like brothers, you know? Which was why I've blamed myself for his death for such a long time. He was supposed to wait for me and for backup while I chased down one of the other fleeing gang members, but instead, he went into the building anyway. And I've been living with the guilt that I shouldn't have left him on his own. We were partners. I should've been there to protect him."

"But surely it's not your fault if he didn't wait for you?"

He nodded. "I know that now. But it's taken me a long time to come to grips with his death and to stop blaming myself. This is why I couldn't tell you before how I feel about you."

"But…"

He lifted her chin. "Somehow I never quite manage to protect the people I love. I want to be with you, but I'm not marrying material. I'm no husband, no dad; I don't know what a family is. I could never give you that. But I want to be with you for as long as I breathe."

With his heart in his throat, Blake stared at Lindsay. He'd seen every emotion while he'd told her he loved her. He'd also seen the bleakness return when he'd tried to explain why he could never marry her. What else was there to say to make her understand?

For while it was quiet in the room before she looked at him. "So how do you think this would work? Do I stay with you? Or do you stay with me? Or do we take turns? And for how long?"

Oh, hell, he was making a mess of things. "We'll live together wherever you want."

"So as if we're married, but we're not?"

This was a trick question, he was sure of it. But for the life of him, he didn't know how to answer it and not say the wrong thing. Because obviously, he was doing this all wrong. "Yeah, kinda."

"So let me get this straight—you love me, you want to be with me, but you don't want to marry me. And the reason why you feel you can't marry anyone is because you didn't have a 'normal' family growing up—whatever 'normal' is. Is that about it?"

He opened and closed his mouth a few times. That was about it. He nodded.

She slowly got up and looked him in the eye. "I love you too, Blake. And granted, I didn't grow up in the system as you did, but I've also lost people I loved. And after Mark, I thought for a long time I could never trust my own feelings again. I really struggled with that, but I fell in love with you anyway. And it was so different, so big, I didn't have a choice but to give my heart to you. I would love to be with you, but I can't do that on a temporary basis."

"It wouldn't be temporary!" he said and tried to catch her hand, but she moved away. "I'll never leave you. But I don't know what it means to be a family, a husband, a dad…"

"You're leaving an escape clause for yourself. At least be honest about it."

He could feel his world crumbling around him but he had no idea how to stop it. "That's not true!"

But she was already at the door. For a moment, he thought she would leave without saying anything more, but then she turned and look at him again. "The reason you don't want to marry me is BS, and you know it. Whatever else you need to know about family and love, I can teach you, Blake. We can teach each other. But that's obviously not what you want. Goodbye."

And then she left, taking his heart with him.

He was still staring dumbfounded at the door when there was a knock. He got up as quickly as he could. Had Lindsay returned? But it was Jason who opened the door. "Are you two decent?" he asked, looking around as he entered with Logan and Charlie just behind him.

"Where's Lindsay?" Charlie asked as she put a tray with coffees next to his bed.

Blake rubbed his face. "She left."

Stunned, everyone stared at him.

"I told her I loved her, damn it! But I don't know how to be a husband or a dad; I can't marry anyone. But I want to be with her."

Charlie rounded on him, her eyes mere slits. "You egotistical idiot! And you told her that? After she'd spent the last twenty hours not knowing how seriously you've been injured, not sleeping, not before she's seen you? Do you have any idea what she'd been through? What exactly did you tell her?"

"I grew up in the system," he got out. "Until Miss Betty took me in when I was twelve."

"Oh, so she made your life miserable?" Charlie wanted to know.

"No! She gave me a real home. But then…she died."

Charlie glared at him. "You think you're the only one who's lost someone close to him? Lindsay and I lost both our parents in one day!"

"She told me. But you two know what it means to be a family; I never had that. I wouldn't know how to protect my family."

"Ah," Charlie snarled. "So, there it is. You're still worried you can't protect Lindsay?"

He opened his mouth to disagree, but realized she was right.

"In case you didn't notice, Lindsay is quite capable of protecting herself. Come on, Logan. I have to find my sister."

With an apologetic smile, Logan followed her. At the

door, she turned around. "I don't know your whole story and I can't imagine what it must have been like to be moved from one foster home to another. But you've been focusing so much on what you didn't have, I think you've missed what you actually had."

Resignedly, he looked at her. It was clear Charlie hadn't quite finished with him. "And what is that?"

"If I'm not mistaken, you and Miss Betty loved each other, you lived together, she took care of you. That's family, that's how families operate. So your excuse doesn't work, I'm afraid. What you do know about love, she taught you. You just never realized it."

It was quiet in the room after Charlie and Logan had left.

"Well, hell," Blake finally said.

"Man, you really made a mess of things, didn't you?" Jason chuckled. "Come on, get dressed. It's time you get home so that you can breathe in some fresh Montana air. Maybe that'll help you to see straight."

"But the doctor..." Blake began but Jason's grin broadened.

"We had to keep you here until Lindsay arrived. I was hoping we'd be celebrating by now, but then you managed to screw up the whole thing anyway. He doesn't know you'll be flying today, not sure what he'd say about that."

"I'll be okay. Won't be the first time I fly after surgery. Only problem is, I don't have clothes."

"I've brought you some clothes from home," Jason said, and for the first time, Blake noticed his black overnight bag on the floor. "Come on, we have a flight to catch." He looked at his watch. "And just for your information, there is time to stop at a jewelry store—just say the word. And the Snowflake Festival in Alisson doesn't end until Sunday. I've heard there's more dancing tomorrow night. You might get another chance with Lindsay if you're lucky. Although, at this point my money is on the vet. And, shame, you're old and injured and would probably have to sit it out anyway. But hey, it's Christmas. You never know, miracles may happen."

Blake managed to throw one of the pillows at Jason, of course, at the exact time the nurse from hell opened the door.

"Managed to chase away your Lindsay, I see?" She snickered, pointing to the pillow on the floor. "Because she wouldn't take your nonsense. I think I like her. Sassy." She picked up his bag and took out a shirt. "Come on, I'll help you get dressed. You need to go get her. Otherwise you'll be miserable for the rest of your life."

For the first time, he noticed the twinkle in her eyes. Docile, he let her help him get dressed while his brain was working overtime.

CHAPTER 18

Inside the big airport terminal, Lindsay looked around for a coffee shop. She couldn't decide whether she was nauseous or hungry. Probably hungry. She hadn't eaten since she'd heard the news about Blake. And she was mad. Hopping mad, truth be told.

Great, straight ahead was one. Hopefully, they'd have a table for one. She'd probably always need a table for one. Better get used to the idea.

"Linds!" a voice called, and as she turned around, she noticed her sister and Logan at a distance. Charlie's hand was on her belly as they rushed closer, and Lindsay groaned out loud. Her sister was pregnant and here she was, only thinking about herself.

"I'm sorry. I should've let you know where I was, but I was just so…"

"Mad?" Charlie said, out of breath.

"Exactly."

"Well"—Logan grinned—"your sister told Blake a thing or two. The poor sod didn't know what hit him."

Lindsay's eyes widened. Charlie rarely got angry. "What did you say?"

"Can we please find a table first? I don't about the rest

of you, but I'm hungry," Charlie said.

"We don't have that much time," Logan said, looking at his watch. "Let's check in and I'll find us a nice table in one of the lounges."

What felt like hours later, they were finally seated in one of the lounges and could eat something.

"Mmm, I needed that," groaned Lindsay after the first bite.

"I told Logan he's an idiot," Charlie said.

Lindsay shrugged. "He has his reasons. I told him it's BS, by the way."

"Good for you." Charlie giggled.

"Can I just please point out something?" Logan asked. "From a male perspective?"

"Please do," Lindsay said.

"Men process things differently and maybe not as quickly as women do. Give the guy's mind time to catch up with his heart. From personal experience"—he grinned and kissed his wife's hand—"I know it takes a while."

Lindsay sighed. "I'm afraid he's persuaded himself he shouldn't ever marry, but I think it's just a way to make sure there is a way out if things don't turn out the way he thought they would."

Grinning, Logan got up. "Give the guy a break, will you? You two Wilsons are a force to behold. Come on, gals, time to board."

"Well," Charlie whispered to Lindsay as they followed Logan out of the lounge, "there are ways and means to persuade them otherwise, you know?"

Lindsay shook her head. "I don't want to have to 'persuade' anyone to love me. I've told Blake I love him. And it wasn't enough."

As they were about to queue to board the plane, Lindsay looked around for the bathroom. Now she was definitely nauseous. She'd probably eaten too quickly.

"Charlie…" she began and swallowed.

Charlie gave her one look before she grabbed her hand.

"Over here, Linds. Logan, give us a minute!" Charlie called to her husband.

They just made it to the bathroom.

"Business class?" Blake asked in surprise as they were shown their seats.

"Logan bought the tickets." Jason grinned. "I didn't complain."

"I'll reimburse him," Blake said, taking his seat. He'd never considered flying business class before even though he could afford it.

"My seat is more to the front," Jason said. "See you in Bozeman."

Blake patted his pocket. It was still there. He'd been such an idiot. Of course, he wanted to marry Lindsay; what the hell had he been thinking? The idea of a future without her in it was simply too awful to contemplate. He didn't want a way out; he wanted to be with her until his last breath. Why the hell hadn't he told her so?

Behind him, more people arrived.

Suddenly Blake heard a very familiar voice. "I think our seats are over here, Charlie."

It was Logan. Which meant Lindsay had to be close by. With his heart hammering away, Blake turned his head. Logan and his wife and Lindsay were coming down the aisle.

He got up, a bit more unsteadily than he'd have liked, and put his hand out to Logan. "I believe you bought the tickets, thank you. I'd like to pay you back."

Grinning, Logan slapped him on his good shoulder. "The least of your problems at the moment, I think." He stood to the side so that Charlie could get to her seat. She completely ignored Blake.

And then Lindsay was in front of him. A very pale Lindsay, he noticed. She also ignored him.

"What's wrong?" he asked.

"What a stupid question," Charlie muttered, but he barely heard her, his whole attention focused on Lindsay.

"Where is your seat?" he asked Lindsay.

She looked down at her phone before she pointed towards the seat next to him. "I can try and change seats…"

But he took her hand. He was given another chance. "Please don't. I…I have to talk to you…"

"I don't think you have anything more to say that I want to listen to," she said as she took her seat.

"Can I get you anything?" he asked.

She opened and closed her mouth before she nodded. "Water will be nice, thanks."

He found the flight attendant and got a bottle of water from her before they closed the plane's doors. Lindsay was staring out of the window when he returned. "Here you go," he said, handing the bottle to her as he took his seat.

"Thanks."

"You're very pale. Please tell me what's wrong?"

"What could possibly be wrong?" she asked in a voice laced with sarcasm. "I'm fine," she added curtly and took another sip of the water.

"Damn it, Lindsay…"

"You love me but you don't want to marry me—I got the message. I don't think any more talking will change the outcome."

"Can we start over, please? I've f—I've messed up. But I love you and I need you to give me another chance."

But Lindsay wouldn't meet his eyes. "We have to sit next to one another for the next three hours. If you have something to say, say it. It doesn't mean I'll listen."

The staff went through the usual rituals while the plane took off. Blake willed himself to relax. Lindsay was here. Next to him. And he had three hours.

He'd never liked being the center of attention, and by now he knew Lindsay well enough to know she also preferred to stay in the background, but if she didn't want to listen to him, he was quite happy to get out of his comfort zone this one time. If forced, he could put on a performance. And if she was going to be embarrassed, it was just too damn bad.

If the only way to get her to listen to him was to make a scene, then he was going to make a spectacular one.

Lindsay kept her eyes closed. At least she was feeling much better. She couldn't remember ever being sick. What a horrible feeling. Must have been something she'd eaten in the lounge.

And now she had to endure the next three hours sitting next to Blake. Even though the armrest between the two seats was quite wide, she became more and more aware of him every time she breathed. She noticed everything about him: the hairs on his arms, his big, muscled legs stretched out in front of him, his beautiful hands. His mere presence and the warmth radiating in her direction were driving her crazy.

Damn it, she'd thought she would have time to prepare herself before she had to face him again. She knew Logan had bought return tickets for all of them, but because she'd been so mad and upset, the thought that Blake might be travelling with them simply hadn't occurred to her.

Finally, the plane was in the air, and the sound of the flight attendant coming down the aisle could be heard. Great, champagne was just what she needed to make the next few hours bearable.

"Bubbly?" the blond flight attendant asked chirpily, fluttering her eyelashes at Blake.

Lindsay gnashed her teeth. Seriously. If it wasn't enough to have been told he didn't want to marry her, she now had to watch him flirt with a ditzy blonde?

Blake took two glasses from the blonde, but he put both in front of him.

"My glass?" Lindsay asked, holding out her hand.

"In a minute," Blake said patting his pockets. "Told you I need to talk to you."

"And I told you I..." But before she could finish her sentence, Blake stood up and moved so that he was right in front of her.

He flashed the flight attendant a killer smile. "I need a few minutes." And before Lindsay could blink, he went down on his knee, opening a small box he was holding in his hand as he knelt down.

Around them people inhaled sharply, exclaimed, and giggles erupted, but Lindsay was so stunned she barely registered the sounds. She couldn't believe what she was seeing—Blake going down on one knee in front of all these strangers? As she very well knew, he didn't like drawing attention to himself.

Although he was smiling, he was cradling his injured arm close to his body, his face paler than usual. She'd been so intent on not talking to him, she wouldn't let herself think about his injury.

"Blake, what are you doing? Your shoulder..."

But his brown eyes remained steadily on her. He ignored the other passengers who had their cell phones out and were recording the whole thing. "Lindsay Wilson, I love you. I can't picture my life without you in it. I don't know how to be a husband, but I know you will teach me. Please marry me?"

Lindsay was seeing stars in front of her and realizing she'd lost her breath upon hearing "Lindsay Wilson." She inhaled deeply. As usual, he'd used no unnecessary words, but he'd actually used more than one word. No long, drawn-out declaration of love from him, just the basics. Exactly what she needed to know.

And there, in the depths of his eyes, she saw also the love he'd professed twice now, saw that he meant what he was saying.

Her gaze dropped to the ring he was holding in his hand. Her heart melted. Somehow, she'd found someone who got her, who understood the wiring of her mind, who knew exactly what kind of ring she'd like. Nestled in the exquisite, dainty clasps of a rose-gold ring, a beautiful solitaire diamond winked at her.

"If you don't like it, we can get another one," Blake said quickly.

Looking at him with her heart in her eyes, she moved forward, got on her knees in front of him, and held out her left hand.

Uncertain, he looked at her hand, then at her. "Is that a yes?"

"Hell, yes, it's a yes!" someone yelled and everyone around them laughed.

But Blake was still watching her, waiting for her answer.

"Yes, Blake, of course I'll marry you, anytime, any place. I love you." She smiled.

"She said yes!" someone else called out, and a huge cheer went up.

He took out the ring, and taking her hand in his, slowly slipped the ring on her finger. And then his good arm shot out so he could haul her closer, and he kissed her.

There were more whistles and laughter from the other passengers, but Lindsay ignored everything else. She was where she'd dreamed of being—in Blake's arms. Safe. Protected. Warm lips were confirming what he'd just said.

"Linds, are you sure about this?" she heard Charlie's voice and lifted her head. Her sister was standing next to them, clearly still worried. Lindsay quickly got up and gave her hand to Blake to help him up.

"I'm sure." She smiled as Blake put an arm around her.

Charlie sniffed, her eyes filling with tears. "I'm so, so happy for you." She cried and embraced them both. "But you..." She pointed at Blake. "You hurt my sister and you'll have to answer to me."

"Yes, ma'am." Blake grinned.

"Don't you ma'am me," Charlie said haughtily, but

then she smiled and hugged them again. "I can't wait to tell Eleanor and Brooke! Logan, I have a plan…" she said, going back to her seat, already apparently planning a party.

But Lindsay had stopped listening to her sister and pressed her face into Blake's chest.

"You know"—he chuckled softly—"this may be a good time to see whether we can become members."

Still on cloud nine, she looked up at him. "Members of what?"

He pressed his mouth close to her ear. "The mile-high club." His sexy whisper sent delicious tingles down her spine and her body reacted. "I need to be with you. Now."

"But your arm…"

Grinning, he took her hand. "I'm sure we'll find a way."

Minutes later, he was finally able to kiss Lindsay the way he'd been thinking about for three weeks. She opened her mouth for him, her lips warm, and he was instantly hard for her.

"I can't wait," he groaned as his hand found the zipper of her jeans. "This is going to be a quickie."

"My thoughts exactly." She smiled as her hand slipped underneath his light sweater.

Within seconds his fingers found her heat—she was ready for him.

"You'd have to help me," he got out. "I only have one arm."

With a grin, she unbuckled his pants and pulled them down. "My pleasure," she said huskily as her hand closed around him.

"If you do that, this will be over before we've started."

"Let's see if we can do this." She giggled. "Never really noticed exactly how small this place actually is."

But he knew exactly what he'd been craving, and nothing was going to keep him from making love to his fiancée, least of all a cramped bathroom. He had her alone; that was all that counted.

Seconds later, his mouth on hers, he slid into her. "Being with you like this—it's home," he whispered. "I realized it the first time we made love."

"Blake," she whispered brokenly as he gathered her closer. Her head fell back, the movements of her body inciting him to move faster and faster.

The storm that had brewed inside him over the last few weeks erupted, spinning them both out of control until all he could do was to hold on to her softness.

Lindsay tried to comb her hair with her fingers as they walked back to their seats. It was probably in vain. She was sure everybody could see exactly what they'd been up to. But everyone else was either watching movies on the small screen in front of them or busy on their phones. Everyone but Charlie, of course.

Her sister caught her eye, her eyebrows raised in question marks.

Blushing, Lindsay nodded before she quickly took her seat.

"Can't believe you're still blushing after what happened." Blake grinned as he took her hand.

"I can't believe what we've just done," she whispered.

He lifted her left hand and looked at the ring. "You're wearing my ring. I'm hoping this will be a regular occurrence."

Still blushing, she nodded. "So do I."

"You sure you're okay with the ring? Because we can always get one more to your liking. I just needed to get one so that you'll know I'm serious. This one reminded me of you—exquisite, elegant, one of its kind."

"The ring was what finally convinced me," she said softly. "When I saw it, I knew you get me."

His eyes darkened and he leaned forward. "I have to

kiss you again."

"Of course," she whispered before she leaned forward so that his lips could claim hers again.

The day, which had started out so dreadfully, had turned into one she'd never forget.

CHAPTER 19

Saturday morning just before noon, Lindsay finally joined Lilly at their booth on the town square. Blake was with her and Lilly's gaze immediately went to their clasped hands.

"You two look happy." She smiled.

Lindsay held up her left hand. It took Lilly a beat to notice the ring, but the next moment, her shriek could be heard all over town.

"Ooooh! I knew it! Congratulations, you two—I just don't know why it took you so long."

"I've just heard!" someone called.

She and Blake looked at each other. "Eleanor," they said in unison, and Blake laughed. They'd been wondering how long it was going to take before Eleanor knew about their engagement.

"Lindsay, Blake!" Eleanor laughed as she arrived, out of breath. She embraced both of them. "I've just finished speaking to Charlie and she told me the whole story." She looked over her shoulder to where Brooke was standing at her own booth. "Brooke! Come here—such great news!"

Smiling, Brooke joined them with Connor right behind her. "What's all the excitement about?"

"They're engaged!" Eleanor exclaimed. "Charlie has just told me how Blake got up in front of all the people in the plane, went down on his knee, and proposed to our Lindsay here. And look at the beautiful ring. Did you ask Lindsay what she liked?" she asked Blake.

"There wasn't time." Blake grinned. "I messed up with round one, so when I knew I had another chance, I also knew I had to go all out."

"Well, you did good." Eleanor sighed.

"It's beautiful, isn't it?" Lindsay smiled.

Brooke touched it with a finger. "Oh, Lindsay, I'm so, so happy for you."

"Don't you think it's time you get yourself another one of those?" Eleanor asked her daughter.

Brooke groaned. "Seriously, Mother. Focus on these two, please?"

"Is that why Blake keeps kissing Lindsay?" Connor asked, and everyone laughed.

Blake kneeled in front of the boy. "It is. One day you'll find someone you want to kiss all the time, as well."

"Yuck, not me," Connor declared quickly. "Mom, can I go and play?"

"May I." Brooked chuckled. "Of course." She turned to Blake and Lindsay as Connor skipped away. "So what are your plans?"

Lindsay looked up at Blake. They'd arrived back quite late last night and by that time, Blake looked very pale. He wouldn't hear of sleeping without her and only agreed to get into bed if she would join him. And then she'd made a new discovery about her fiancé—no bullet was going to keep him from making love to her again. So they hadn't really talked about any future plans yet.

"We're still enjoying just being engaged. There's plenty of time for plans." Blake smiled before he bent down and kissed her. "I'm going to get my stuff at home. I'll see you later."

A little taken aback, Lindsay stared after him. Could it

be he was having second thoughts?

"Oh, Lindsay, you're here, I'm so glad!" Lindsay turned around to see Suzie Stevens making her way through the throng of people towards Lindsay's booth, her hand clutching the arm of the woman who was next to her.

"This is my sister, Mabel," Suzie said, out of breath when she reached the booth. "Her husband is having the same problem," she whispered loudly.

"Well then, you've come to the right place." Lindsay smiled.

But Eleanor wasn't quite finished yet. "You know, a Christmas wedding is very special."

Brooke rolled her eyes and grabbed her mother's arm. "Mother, what am I going to do with you? They will make their own plans. Come on, I need your help." And with a wink in Lindsay's direction, she took her mother away. "We'll see you tonight!"

"Lindsay?" Suzie asked again and Lindsay smiled. She was being paranoid. Blake hadn't said anything strange. He'd told her he loved her, he'd given her a ring; of course there wasn't any rush to make plans just yet. Maybe he wanted to wait until after Christmas?

Monday morning early when Blake woke up, Lindsay wasn't next to him. Frowning, he got up. Now that he thought about it, he'd also woken up alone yesterday morning.

There were sounds coming from the bathroom. She was probably getting ready for work. Struggling with his one hand, he pulled on his jeans and headed down the stairs. Lindsay loved her coffee first thing in the morning, he'd discovered.

As he put on the coffee machine, he saw a cup of tea on the counter. Strange, he'd seldom seen her drink tea. But okay, so sometimes she preferred tea. While he waited for the coffee, he walked towards the window. He'd brought some of his stuff here, but there wasn't that much space in Lindsay's bedroom.

They had so much to talk about and to decide, but because he was keeping Christmas a surprise for her, he'd been evading her questions. It would definitely be the last time he kept anything from her; it was killing him not to blurt out everything that was going on. It was clear to him she was slightly miffed because he wouldn't discuss any plans with her, but all would be revealed soon.

He heard the ping of the coffee machine behind him but as he turned, he saw the garage doors opened. And the next minute, Lindsay was driving down the driveway and turning into the street.

Nonplussed, he stared at the car driving away. She hadn't said anything last night about leaving early. Besides, she had to know he was in the kitchen.

His phone. It was still in the bedroom. He raced up the stairs and picked up his phone from the bed. Yes, there was a message from Lindsay.

On my way to work. See you later! ☺

What the hell? They were engaged, they'd made love not so long ago, so why had she just left without telling him?

Something was wrong. His gut had been telling him precisely that for the last twenty-four hours, but he should've listened to it and not simply ignored it.

Over the weekend, Lindsay had been quiet and she'd slept most of yesterday. He'd put it down to all the stress of the past few months. And he hadn't minded the rest; his arm had been giving him hell after Friday's flight, and of course making love to his fiancée in the small bathroom hadn't been conducive to keeping his arm still. But it had been so worth it.

But he should've asked her if something was wrong last night. He should've made sure she was okay.

Within minutes, he was in his car, driving towards Lindsay's shop.

Stunned, Lindsay walked out of the doctor's office. Charlie, who was waiting for her outside, rushed closer when she saw her. "Linds? What's wrong? What did the doctor say?"

"Nothing is wrong…" she began, but before she could say anything else, the door burst open and in strode Blake—a furious one, if she wasn't mistaken.

He yanked her close to him and buried his face in her neck for a moment. Inhaling deeply, he cupped her face. "Lindsay, damn it, why are you at the doctor's? And why the hell didn't you tell me where you were going? Why didn't you tell me you were feeling ill? We're engaged, damn it. I love you! But—"

Taking a deep breath, she interrupted him. "I just have to check something with you first before I tell you." She had no idea how he was going to react to the news. When he'd asked her to marry him, he hadn't said anything about kids, and since they'd gotten engaged, he wouldn't talk about any plans for the future. Well, the sooner she knew, the better.

"What?" he barked out.

"Do you still want to marry me?"

"Of course, I want to marry you—I gave you a damn ring."

"But you don't want to talk about plans."

His mouth opened and closed before he rubbed his face. "Because damn it, I wanted it to be a surprise for you."

"A surprise?" She laughed, feeling a little hysterical. "Well, it's good to know you like surprises, because do I have a surprise for you."

"What surprise?"

"I'm pregnant," she blurted out, and waited.

"I told you that's why you were so tired!" Charlie laughed and hugged her, but Lindsay kept her eyes on

Blake.

One emotion after the other passed over his face until she saw the one she'd been hoping for, waiting for—joy.

Reverently, he touched her belly, his eyes shimmering with tears. Tears. Her Blake in tears. "You're pregnant? With our baby?"

"Yes. I'm pregnant with our baby."

"Damn woman, I love you," he said, and lifting her up with his good arm, proceeded to kiss her soundly.

"What the hell are you doing with my sister?" a voice thundered close by.

Lindsay turned around and blinked. Gavin? What was he doing here? He was supposed to be arriving next week.

But Charlie had thrown her arms around their brother and was hugging him and crying at the same time. "I'm so happy, I can't believe this. Linds is pregnant and now you're here."

Her words only deepened the frown on Gavin's face. "Lindsay is *what*?" Gavin asked, his eyes narrowing as he stared at Blake.

"Pregnant. And I'm so happy you're here!" Lindsay called out as she embraced her brother.

Gavin looked down at her. "I'm gone for a few weeks and now my other sister is also pregnant? What's in the water of this place?" He put his hands on her shoulders. "You sure you're happy?"

"Very." She smiled.

"Well, in that case," said Gavin, "I suppose I have to congratulate the dad." He walked over to Blake and held out his hand.

Both she and Charlie held their breaths. Gavin had been known for his death grip on any potential boyfriend of theirs in the past. But Blake didn't blink, just shook hands and smiled.

"So, what are your plans with my sister?" Gavin asked.

"I'm going to marry her."

"Good answer," said Gavin and finally chuckled.

"When?"

"It's a surprise for Lindsay," Blake said, moving closer to Lindsay. "And now I'm taking my fiancée home."

"I have to get to the shop…"

"Later," he said.

The look in his eye robbed her of her breath and she could only nod. He wanted her. By now she knew that light in his eyes. She couldn't wait, either. The need to be with him after the overwhelming news was…overwhelming.

And she also needed a minute to get used to the idea she was going to be a mother.

She quickly hugged Charlie and Gavin. "Have you been to the house?" she asked Gavin.

"No, I went to your shop and Charlie's rooms directly from the airport. Imagine how I felt when Lilly told me both my sisters were at the doctor's."

"You could've let us know you were on your way." Charlie laughed. "Why don't you come with me to the ranch? I've brought Linds to the doctor, so my car is here and she clearly has another lift. There's plenty of room and Logan would love to see you. That way you can give these two lovebirds some space. We actually have a proposition for you."

Lindsay threw Charlie a grateful look as she and Blake left. She was so happy her brother was back, but there hadn't been time to clean his room.

"A good thing your brother has another place to stay." Blake chuckled as they walked towards his car. He had his arm around her and bent down. "You're a very loud lover."

Blushing, she put her hands against her face. "I'm not the only one."

They were halfway to his car, but Blake stopped and kissed her, right there in the middle of the street for all to see. In an hour's time the whole town would probably know that one, she and Blake was engaged; two, she was pregnant; and three, Gavin was back.

But she couldn't be happier. And maybe now that he knew a baby was on the way, Blake might just want to talk about wedding plans.

CHAPTER 20

Charlie clapped her hands. "This is the one, don't you agree, Eleanor? Brooke? What do you think?"

Lindsay stared at herself in the mirror. It was a beautiful dress in champagne-colored lace enhanced by layers of misty tulle and organza, which added texture to the A-line silhouette. Beaded spaghetti straps balanced the sweetheart neckline of the semi-sheer bodice while more lace cascaded down the entire length of the soft skirt. It was perfect, and Blake would love the lace.

And if she'd known when she'd be getting married, she'd buy the dress in a heartbeat, but for some or other reason her fiancé refused to talk about wedding plans. Every time she mentioned it, he mumbled something about a surprise but she had yet to discover what the surprise was.

The last few days had been crazy. Her days were busy in the shop and she'd looked forward to spending time with Blake in the evenings, but each night he'd told her he had things to do. She'd hardly seen him. She had enough to keep her busy and she could hardly keep up with mixing enough creams for her shop, but she missed him.

"Oh, it's perfect." Brooke sighed.

"I love it," Eleanor said, her eyes full of tears.

"What do you think, Linds?" Charlie wanted to know.

Lindsay turned away from the mirror and tried to open the row of tiny buttons at her back. "It's a lovely dress, but I have no idea when we're getting married. How did we end up in a bridal shop anyway? I thought we were Christmas shopping?"

"We are, but we happened to see this bridal shop, and seeing that we have a bride-to-be with us, it makes sense to try on wedding dresses." Charlie smiled.

"I still can't believe you talked me into joining you today to go Christmas shopping in Bozeman." Lindsay smiled, trying to get out of the dress. "It's three days before Christmas and it's the busiest time of year in the shop."

"There's always time for fun," Eleanor said.

Charlie helped her with the dress. "And now it's time for lunch, what do you all say?"

"Yes, please." Lindsay grinned. "Baby seems to be always hungry."

Charlie patted her own tummy. "Tell me about it."

Outside, Charlie motioned to a coffee shop across the street. "I think I'm going to get that pair of shoes I saw earlier. Get a table for us; I'll be right there."

Shoes? Lindsay frowned and stared after her sister. She couldn't remember Charlie trying on shoes? But Eleanor grabbed her arm. "Come on, I'm hungry!"

On Christmas Eve, Blake stopped in front of Lindsay's shop just as she was locking the door. He'd been counting the days. Thank goodness it was finally time.

When he'd thought of surprising Lindsay today, he definitely hadn't thought of the day-by-day consequences of keeping such a surprise a surprise.

She'd lost her sparkle and he hated that, but hopefully after tonight, the sparkle would be back in her beautiful blue eyes.

The car was packed and they were heading out to Logan's ranch, where everybody would be staying until tomorrow. Gavin had been staying with Logan and Charlie since he'd arrived, and Eleanor, Brooke, and Connor would probably also spend a few more days on the ranch after Christmas. But he had plans to whisk Lindsay away to sunshine, long beaches, and longer nights.

As she walked towards him, his heart simply tumbled to the ground. He loved this woman, and each day he thanked his lucky stars she loved him right back.

"Hi, beautiful." He smiled and hugged her close.

"Thank you for saying that, but after this day, I really don't feel beautiful. I can't wait to put up my feet." She smiled and hugged him back. "Where's the sling?" she asked, surprised, and touched his arm. "Stiches out?"

"Yep, so now I can use both hands again." He grinned and stroked her back with both his hands.

She nestled close to him. "Mmm, I'll fall asleep right here if you continue. But we better get a move on; Charlie has been phoning all afternoon."

Fifteen minutes later, they stopped in front of the lovely homestead on Logan's ranch.

Lindsay bent to pick up her bag, but he stopped her. It was time to tell her about the surprise. "I have a question."

"Yeah?" she asked absentmindedly while picking up her bag.

"You remember you agreed to marry me?"

She stilled before she looked at him. "Yes?"

He could see in her eyes she was beginning to suspect something. "And you did say at any time, any place, if I remember correctly?"

"Yes?" she whispered.

"So how about we get married on this ranch, tomorrow?"

For long minutes she stared at him while every single emotion she was feeling passed over her face in rapid succession. And then she smiled—a wide grin that told him all he needed to know.

"Of course, I'll marry you!" she cried out and leaned forward for a kiss. But his lips had barely touched hers when she lifted her head. "But how? I don't even have a dress?"

The door on her side flew open and Charlie laughed. "Yes, you do! Remember the one you tried on in Bozeman a few days ago?"

Lindsay looked at him before her head swiveled back to Charlie. "You knew about this and you didn't tell me?"

"Yes!" Charlie called out. "I could burst with wanting to tell you, but we promised."

"We?" Lindsay said. "You mean to tell me…"

"Yip." Charlie grinned, motioning towards the house. "We all knew."

And standing on the porch was everybody Lindsay called family, and who were now also his family.

"And you have the dress?" she asked Charlie.

"I have the dress."

Lindsay hugged her sister while she searched for Blake's eyes. He still looked at her, a little unsure. She waited until everyone had entered the house before she took his hand. "Thank you."

"You sure you're okay with this?"

"I'm getting married without the usual hassles—of course, I'm sure."

"Good answer." He grinned as they stepped into the house.

By eight o'clock they were all gathered in the dining room. The table was beautifully laid with Charlie's best china, and Christmas decorations. In the corner, the huge Christmas tree was lit up, giving the big room that special warm-and-fuzzy Christmas feeling.

Lindsay sighed and caught Charlie and Gavin's eyes.

They were all thinking of Christmas days past when their parents had been still alive.

But Charlie patted her eyes with a tissue and smiled. "No tears tonight—we have so much to be thankful for and to celebrate."

Logan got up and cleared his throat. "We have several announcements to make before we eat."

"Really?" Eleanor called out. "Does it have to be now with the food in front of us? I don't know about the rest of you but I'm hungry."

"One of the announcements concerns you, Mom." Logan grinned.

Warily, she looked first at Logan and then at Brooke. "You're not going to put me in an old age home, are you?"

Everyone burst out laughing and Logan shook his head. "They'll send you back. I won't dare," he joked. "Besides, we want you close to us, and I'll get to that in a little while. But first things first. We've decided on a name for our baby girl."

Eleanor's eyes immediately filled with tears. "Yes?" she breathed.

"She's going to have her grandma's name!" Charlie called out just as Logan opened his mouth.

He tried to look sternly at his wife, but she got up and kissed him. "You were taking way too long. She'll be Eleanor, but we'll call her Ellie."

Eleanor clutched her chest with both hands. "Oh, how wonderful," she sniffed. "I'm so happy. Ellie. What a beautiful name."

"It means 'shining light,'" Charlie said. "Like her grandma."

While Eleanor looked for a tissue in her bag, Brooke smiled. "So what other announcements do you have?"

"Well," Logan said, taking Charlie's hand. "Charlie and I have been talking. We have this big ranch and we'd like to share it with you. That is, of course, if you want to. Blake has already agreed—part of his surprise for you,

Lindsay, so I'll leave it to him to explain. But Mom and Brooke, and of course, Gavin, we'd like all of you to come and stay on the ranch. Everyone would have his or her own house, of course. But we'll be together and this way, Mom, you can see your granddaughter whenever you like."

"Think about it," Charlie said. "You don't have to decide right now, but I can't think of anything nicer than to have all of you close by. But now, let's eat!"

By this time, Lindsay's head was reeling.

Blake took her hand. "Say something? Will you be okay with living here on the ranch close to your sister and brother?"

Still stunned, Lindsay nodded. "I can't think of anything more wonderful, but how? And when? I...I don't..."

Smiling, Blake kissed her. "Logan reached out with the suggestion that we build our own house on the ranch. I know how close you and Charlie are..."

"But what about you? Are you okay with the idea of staying on Logan's farm?"

"I simply want to be where you are. Besides, thanks to Miss Betty, I was able to invest in the ranch, so now we own part of it."

"Really?"

"Really. Our house isn't finished, though, but we have a bedroom for tonight, and tomorrow night before I whisk you away on our honeymoon, we'll spend the night there together."

Shaking her head, Lindsay laughed. "Well, my head is spinning. It's a good thing I love surprises, isn't it?"

"A very good thing." He grinned and took her hand. "You sure about marrying me?"

"Of course. I love you."

He cupped her face. "I love you, too."

"Hey, you two," Charlie called out. "You're going to need food at some point. Please eat."

Lindsay caught Blake's eye. She wasn't hungry for food

and neither, it would seem, was her fiancé.

He leaned over to her. "Do you want to see our new house?"

He heart leaped up and she nodded. "Yes, please."

Logan got up. "Excuse us, I'm going to show Lindsay our new home."

"Okay! I'll keep your food!" Charlie called after them.

Late the next morning, Logan waved as Lindsay walked towards the big homestead. Charlie had been calling Lindsay's phone for the last hour, but each time she'd tried to get up, he'd managed to get her to stay in bed just a little longer.

He stared after his fiancée. He would probably never understand exactly why he'd been given this chance at love, but he was going to do everything in his power to always love and protect Lindsay.

Logan and Gavin appeared around the corner.

"I don't have to ask whether you had a good night— it's written all over your face." Logan grinned as they came closer. "Hopefully, by the time you're back from your honeymoon, we should be finished with the kitchen."

"I don't know how to thank you," Blake said. "There wouldn't even have been a room without your help."

"You've paid for it all." Logan grinned.

"You've made it possible." Blake had to swallow a few times before he could speak again. "Never thought I'd be part of a family."

Logan slapped him on the shoulder. "Great to have you here. I'm also hoping you'll help us with a new security system?"

"Of course. We'll discuss it when we're back."

"So, Gavin, what about you?" Logan asked Lindsay and Charlie's brother. "We're really hoping you'll also settle here. I know Charlie would love to have both you and Lindsay close by."

Gavin nodded. "Thank you. But for now, I'll stay in Charlie's house in town until I figure out what's next. I still have work to do for the firm in South Africa…"

"But you are considering my proposal to join my firm?" Logan asked.

Gavin nodded. "Yes, but I need time."

"Of course. Come on, Blake, I want to talk to you about the kitchen."

"I thought we'd ask Lindsay about color schemes, but what do you think about having a big window here, overlooking the ranch?" Logan asked.

Blake joined Logan and stared out over the rolling hills where horses were grazing in the distance.

Home. Family. A place to call his own. His and Lindsay's. His body felt too small for all the emotion, and he had to inhale deeply.

The next day, Lindsay's heart was in her throat as she walked towards her bridegroom, beside her brother, her arm linked through his. She had a hard time not rushing down the short aisle in Logan and Charlie's spacious sitting room.

When she'd joined her sister, and Eleanor and Brooke, and just about everyone else from town just before lunch, they were already in the process of transforming the large dining room and lounge into a wedding venue.

Everyone had pitched in. Some were cooking, others were doing the flowers, others laid the tables while the men made sure fairy lights went up just about everywhere. She felt so lucky to be part of such a caring community.

"I can always get you out of here," Gavin said, under his breath.

"I'm right where I want to be." She grinned. "I'm so happy you're here. Thanks for your support."

"Of course." He cleared his throat. "Mom and Dad would've been so proud of you, Linds."

She hugged his arm, tears threatening to spill. Oh, how she wished they could've been here today. Her dad would've loved Blake's quiet way of doing things, and her mom would've made a remark about her handsome, new son-in-law.

Swallowing against the lump in her throat, she laughed with everyone as Blake began to walk towards them.

"You're taking way too long to get my bride to me, Gavin." He grinned and caught her hand.

"You make her happy, or..." Gavin said, his voice not quite steady, and this time Blake did wince as they shook hands.

"I will," he promised before he turned towards her.

"Beautiful," he murmured and bent his head. "You look so beautiful."

"The kiss is only supposed to be much later." She giggled.

"I can't wait any longer," he said, and kissed her.

Lindsay was out of breath and laughing by the time they'd finished dancing to her song about crazy and beautiful. Blake had danced her out onto the porch, and when the music stopped, he took her hand. "Come with me? I've told Charlie we're leaving. You'll see them all tomorrow morning before we leave.

"So are we having our honeymoon in our new home? Surely you can tell me now?" she asked as they started to walk down the short road to their house.

"We're sleeping there tonight, but then, beautiful, I'm taking you far away to an island in the sun."

"It sounds perfect."

In front of the half-finished house, she stopped and caught her breath. "Did you put the fairy lights on the porch?"

"Of course." He smiled. "It had to be like it was in my dream."

"What dream?" she asked as she leaned against him, staring at the lights.

"The one of us with two little girls with their mother's clear blue eyes and a boy with dark hair. There were fairy lights on the porch, just like there are now. Oh, and we have to get a dog. A spaniel."

She laughed. "A spaniel. That's very precise."

He turned her around to face him. "I saw them all so clearly. And I promise, I'll always be there, protecting you all."

"Of course, you will. Take me to our bed, husband?"

"Yes, Mrs. Davidson," he said as he led her up the half-finished porch to their bedroom.

"Mrs. Davidson?" She smiled. "Well, have I told you Mrs. Davidson has her own surprise for you?"

"Yeah?"

"You remember the conversation you overheard in my shop with Suzie Stevens?"

He gave her a stern look. "Told you I don't have problems in the bedroom."

"Oh, I know. But I do have something that may just...well...enhance the pleasure," she said as he opened the bedroom door.

She just had time to see his eyes flash before he gathered her close. "Enhance the pleasure? So how are you going to do that?"

"Well, I remember you like ylang-ylang..." she began, but he bent down and kissed her. It was going to be a while before she could take out the lovely massage cream she'd made just for him.

ACKNOWLEDGEMENTS

A heartfelt thanks to Melissa Keir and Inkspell Publshing for this one – it's such a priviledge to work with you.

I'd also like to thank each and every reader who take the time to pick up one of my stories, reach out with a message or submit a review – you have no idea how it warms my heart.

And as always, thanks to Theo, my husband who after all this time, still diligently reads my words and keeps cheering me on from the sides – you make it so easy to write about love.

SNEAK PEEK AT THE THIRD BOOK IN THE UNEXPECTED LOVE SERIES

LOVING BROOKE

A kiss? Seriously. Baffled, Brooke put the paintbrush down, her eyes never leaving the painting she'd just finished. She was known for her 'vividly realized, oil, landscape paintings' as an art journal once hailed one of her paintings. And recently, another critic had raved about her work, describing one of her paintings as 'simple, bold forms expressed in strong strokes and richly saturated colors'.

Okay, lately, she'd moved away from only doing landscape painting and had begun to explore the human figure, but what she'd done on this canvas was something entirely different.

This was a kiss. No matter how or from which angle you looked at the finished work in front of her, there was no doubt about the subject matter.

The faces of the couple kissing were shadowy, their features blurry, but they were kissing—that much was clear. Ardently kissing, to be precise. But gone were the 'bold strokes and richly saturated colors'. Instead, muted hues created a dreamlike glow inside of which scratchy brushstrokes swirled around to form lips kissing.

And why did the blurry features look so familiar?

Brooke tried to comb back her hair with unsteady fingers. She hadn't been sleeping well; that was probably the reason she was seeing things that weren't there.

Irritated, she brushed another piece of hair out of her

face. Why was her hair all over the place? Hadn't she put it up in a ponytail this morning? Patting her hair, she tried to find the scrunchie she'd used to put her hair in a ponytail earlier. Where was it? Had she put up her hair this morning? Shaking her head, she dropped her hand. She couldn't even remember as she'd been so wrapped up in getting the restlessness she'd been experiencing over the last few weeks onto a canvas. What she hadn't expected, though, was that the end result would be...a kiss.

***

DON'T MISS THE FIRST BOOK IN THE UNEXPECTED LOVE SERIES...KISSING CHARLIE

One Kiss Will Change Their Lives Forever

Bowen therapist Charlie Wilson is not interested in men or relationships. Her only concern is making sure her sister Lindsay is safe.

But then billionaire Logan Johnson walks into her rooms and stirs powerful feelings inside of her. Logan's perfectly knotted tie is a clear indication free-spirit Charlie should steer clear of him at all costs.

They are complete opposites, so why does he keep coming back to see her?

EXCERPT:

"How did you hurt your back?" Her voice was cool, and she wasn't meeting his eyes.

"While hiking," he said curtly. He was in pain; it didn't matter what the hell happened. "Tell me about this Wowen, Bowen, whatever the hell you call this cr— therapy."

She gave him a cool look. "It's called Bowen Therapy."

"Bowen Therapy," he said, his gaze on her mouth.

"The guiding principles of the technique were established by Tom Bowen during the 1950s. It focuses on the whole person, not just the condition. In other words, it treats the cause, not only the symptoms. It helps the body to heal and restores the balance by shifting the body from your innate 'fight or flight' system to a more natural state of calm."

He watched her as she studied his body. She was holding something in her hand. Damn, she had yet to touch him, but he was struggling not to react to her nearness. The fact that he was lying on his back wasn't helping, either.

"Natural state of calm? With you doing strange things to my body?" he grumbled, only realizing the ambiguity of his words when they hung in the air around them.

Her lips twitched.

"Oh, you think this is funny?" he snarled.

"I think you're in pain. I think you like being in control and at the moment, you're not. That's why you feel the need to lash out. But it's fine. I often have children throwing tantrums."

"I'm not throwing a tantrum, damn it…" He tried to sit up straight, but a pain shot up his back, and groaning, he had to slowly lie down again.

"The movements in Bowen Therapy," she continued as if he hadn't interrupted her, "are very distinctive and are used on precise points on the body. It involves moving the soft tissue in a particular way. I will use a rolling-type movement, using my fingers, hands, or sometimes my elbow. It will create a focus for the brain by stimulating the nerve pathways and tissue. I work on only a small area, depending how far your skin can move. What you may find strange—"

"This whole damn day is strange. I don't know what the hell my mother was thinking," he muttered.

Available Where Books Are Sold...

ABOUT THE AUTHOR

Elsa has been reading love stories for as long as she can remember and when she 'met' the classic authors like Jane Austen, Elizabeth Gaskell, Henry James The Brontë sisters, etc. during her English Honours studies, she was hooked for life.

She married her college boyfriend and soul mate and after 46 years, 3 interesting and wonderful children and 4 beautiful grandchildren, they are now fortunate to live in the picturesque little seaside village of Betty's Bay, South Africa.

She likes the heroines in her stories to be beautiful, feisty, independent and headstrong. And the heroes must be strong but possess a generous amount of sensitivity. They are of course, also gorgeous! Her stories typically incorporate the family background of the characters to better understand where they come from and who they are when we meet them in the story.

Webpage: www.elsawinckler.com
Personal Facebook page:
https://www.facebook.com/elsa.winckler
Author Facebook page:
https://www.facebook.com/ElsaWincklerRomanceAutho r?ref_type=bookmark
Twitter: https://twitter.com/elsawinckler @elsawinckler
Goodreads:
https://www.goodreads.com/author/show/6557709.Elsa _Winckler
Pinterest: http://www.pinterest.com/elsawinckler/
Wattpad: http://www.wattpad.com/user/elsaw1
Instagram: https://www.instagram.com/elsaw1/